Augustin Filon, Janet E. Hogarth, William L. Courtney

The Modern French Drama

Augustin Filon, Janet E. Hogarth, William L. Courtney

The Modern French Drama

ISBN/EAN: 9783337303396

Printed in Europe, USA, Canada, Australia, Japan

Cover: Foto ©Andreas Hilbeck / pixelio.de

More available books at **www.hansebooks.com**

THE MODERN FRENCH DRAMA

Seven Essays

BY

AUGUSTIN FILON

TRANSLATED BY JANET E. HOGARTH

WITH AN INTRODUCTION
BY
W. L. COURTNEY

LONDON: CHAPMAN AND HALL, LIMITED
1898

CONTENTS.

INTRODUCTION.

M. Filon's Essays on the French Drama seem to require no other introduction to a British public than can be contained in a formal explanatory note. Those who have read M. Filon's books, his studies of prominent English statesmen, his novels, above all, his essays on the modern English stage, originally contributed to the *Revue des Deux Mondes*, will know how keen and clear is his critical insight and how skilful is the manipulation of his materials in order to produce the impression which he desires. Without doubt, in his papers published in the *Revue des Deux Mondes*, he did a substantial service to his countrymen, for he was able to explain to them a fact which, through incuriousness or unfamiliarity, they were apt to ignore—

that modern England possessed a stage, supported by dramatic writers of ability, independence, and originality. When the papers on the English Stage first appeared in book form, I asked M. Filon to do something of the same kind of service for English readers as he had already done for his kinsmen across the Channel, and illustrate in the pages of the *Fortnightly Review* some of the main principles and tendencies underlying the contemporary drama in Paris. The conditions in the two cases, I was aware, were not parallel; for I think we may flatter ourselves that we know more about French drama and French literature in London than our neighbours know about literary or dramatic movements in England. But it is one thing to be acquainted with individual plays, and quite another thing to understand the course of theatrical development; and although we speak glibly enough of Augier, of the younger Dumas, of Hervieu, of Lemaître, and still later playwrights in the French capital, we can hardly without assistance understand the relations which they bear to one another, or comprehend the links of sympathy or antagonism which connect the various schools. A work like that of M. Filon gives us, as it seems to me, an important and valuable picture. We may agree with some of the details or may disagree. But in either case we know where we are, and our criticism gains a new aim and meaning.

According to M. Filon there are five distinct movements which explain the modern French Stage, or rather five classifications which we may adopt to interpret its principles and its methods. In the first of these comes the older theatre of Scribe and Sardou, based on a knowledge of theatrical technique, proud above all to produce the "pièce bien faite." To that succeeds the school of Dumas and Augier, adopting the machinery of their predecessors but paying more attention to psychological considerations, and insisting on the portrayal of character as of primary importance. Thus, to use the French nomenclature, we arrive at the "pièce à thèse," the source and origin of all those "problem plays" which had a brief and meteor-like career amongst ourselves. Then follows the curious movement connected with the genius of M.

Antoine and the Théâtre Libre. The problem play, like the well-constructed play, is apt to get into certain mechanical and stereotyped grooves, and the spirit which, for want of a better name, we call the spirit of Naturalism, inaugurates a revolt, bringing with it a newer, more natural, and more spontaneous style of acting, in itself an almost incalculable advantage. We have had nothing correspondent to this in London, for our experiments in a free theatre have, with a very few exceptions, only resulted in productions formless, irregular, and bizarre. The sequel to the movement in Paris may yet, however, be represented amongst ourselves. In process of time the younger French writers discovered that the theatre cannot succeed without certain dramatic conventions, as necessary and as inevitable in the art of Thespis as their analogues have proved to be in the history of Literature. These dramatic conventions, which only inexperienced authors have ever supposed to be irritating and unnecessary obstacles to their industry, began to reappear in Paris at first surreptitiously, afterwards, as psychology gained ground, more openly in such dramatists as De Curel, Hervieu, and Lemaître.

We have got now to the latest phase of French dramatic art, which is nothing more nor less than a real romantic revival. Good, noble, and unselfish characters make their re-appearance. It is recognised that the great body of theatre-goers, who are, perhaps, more conservative than any other section of our modern democratical societies, desire to be emotionally moved by Virtue, and to be emotionally repelled by Vice. There is nothing in our own Metropolis which the pit and the gallery more instinctively admire than the triumph of Goodness and the defeat of Evil; or if this poetic justice be denied them, they at all events require to be shown that, whether they succeed or fail, honesty, justice, and loving kindness are their own exceeding great reward. In Paris the underlying human forces which make for what is pure and beautiful have blossomed forth into the poetical dramas of *Le Chemineau* and *Cyrano de Bergerac*, in both of which, though in the last more obviously than the first, the spectator sees, and loves to see, the old romantic ideals of his youth triumphing over all that is sordid and ugly in a late and materialistic age.

At the date when I am writing, M. Jean Richepin's *Le Chemineau* has already made its appearance in an English guise at Her Majesty's Theatre, while *Cyrano de Bergerac*, with M. Coquelin in the title-rôle, is announced at the Lyceum. It is a tempting subject of inquiry whether in London, too, we shall get in our theatres a resurrection of the romantic and poetical drama. Many indications seem to point that way. Theatrical productions, as a rule, follow movements in novelistic literature, and just as the problem play came as the attendant upon the problem novel, so the undeniable popularity of literary romance at the present day may be succeeded by a similar phenomenon on the stage. It is always unsafe to prophesy, however, and at the end of the theatrical season of 1898 it seems more than usually perilous. For some little time past, so far as the theatre is concerned, we have been moving in a dim world of uncertain ideals; our authors themselves seem not to know what to aim at, because neither their audiences nor the dramatic critics give them any guidance. At the time when the problem play was rife, Mr. Pinero produced the one characteristic and conspicuous drama which has been seen in modern years on London boards. *The Second Mrs. Tanqueray* was a wonderful achievement because it summed up in itself and represented in enduring form characteristic tendencies in our period. It was a much more remarkable triumph than *La Dame aux Camélias*, for while Dumas wrote—with a certain boyish exuberance—his defence of the courtesan, Mr. Pinero's tremendous indictment of the courtesan was composed in the maturity of his powers. Since then, however, he has produced nothing typical with the exception, perhaps, of *The Princess and the Butterfly*, which, with many obvious defects and unnecessary episodes, was, nevertheless, a study in the kind of fantastic comedy of which we have had few examples since Shakespeare. The other and more familiar type of comedy, the comedy of manners, has been brilliantly illustrated by Mr. Henry Arthur Jones in that admirable piece, *The Case of Rebellious*

THE MODERN FRENCH DRAMA.

In the summer of 1895 the *Revue des Deux Mondes* had just begun to publish my studies of the modern English stage, which have attracted some little notice and roused a certain amount of controversy on both sides of the Channel. The Editor of the *Fortnightly Review* thereupon suggested that I should write a similar series of articles on the modern French drama for English readers. In spite of the attractiveness of the proposal, my first instinct was to decline a task for which I did not feel myself properly qualified.

I had several excellent reasons. The first, which makes any enumeration of the others unnecessary, was my complete ignorance of the modern French theatre. In my early youth I had been a most zealous and enthusiastic *habitué* of our leading theatres, but stress of circumstance had exiled me from the world which I loved, and I had never returned to it. It will hardly be credited that for exactly a quarter of a century I had not set foot in the Comédie Française. Not one single Englishman of culture who travels on the Continent could be said to stand where I stood two years ago. What right had I, then, to offer myself as a guide to people whose knowledge went far beyond mine?

Still, I paused to take counsel, and good counsellors came to my assistance. After all, was the disqualification absolute? On the contrary, might one not see in it the distinct leading of destiny? To experience the full shock of an impression, one must return after a long absence. Then the image of the past in all its clearness, completeness, and precision, rises up in the memory to confront the image of the present, and the result is a vivid illuminating realisation of those slow, invisible processes of transformation which are for ever working themselves out both in nature and in Art. If I am the Epimenides, the Rip Van Winkle, of the French drama, my astonished awakening may be worthy of notice, since an awakening is always sincere, and astonishment is often instructive.

The very manner in which I had to approach my subject suggested the adoption of a plan and method exactly contrary to that adopted in my work on the English drama. In France I was addressing a public ignorant even of the existence of the modern English stage, and sufficiently under the sway of ancient prejudice to be disposed to deny that it existed. I was obliged to go back half a century, and to retrace all the different stages through which the English drama has been slowly evolving. There is no such necessity now. My readers will all admit without discussion that throughout this century the French theatre has not only been in existence, but that its existence has been not inglorious ; it is not a history that they want, but a picture.

This, as it happens, is the only thing that I can offer them. Compare that outline sketch of the theatre of Dumas and Augier which remains vividly impressed on my memory, with the impression which I have just received of the dramatic world of 1898—authors, managers, artists, critics, public, and all that appertains to it—and you have my book. Between the two I must insert, by way of the requisite means of transition, a few suggestions as to the origin of the chief features in the existing movement. I shall leave out all that the English reader is likely to know already. I shall also leave out exceptions and eccentricities, literary monstrosities and abnormalities. The foreign reader has neither time nor inclination to acquire more than a very little information about the mazes of his neighbours' literature. All the more necessary is it that that little should be substantial, well chosen, easy of assimilation, and so condensed that the intellectual nourishment which it contains is in inverse proportion to its bulk.

I.

THE AGE OF DUMAS AND AUGIER.

One must first fix the limits of this age. Where did the work of Dumas and Augier begin and end? I can give a very definite answer to this double question. The period in our dramatic history which I wish to describe by this name is bounded by two abortive movements. The Romanticism of 1825—1845 gave France a school of poets and tried vainly to give it a theatre. From 1875 to 1890 Naturalism, which had created a new form of novel, sought to establish itself on the stage: it failed, as Romanticism had failed before it. The thirty or forty years which intervened between these two unsuccessful attempts belong to Augier and Dumas, their contemporaries and their disciples.

At first Dumas had not yet appeared on the scene, and Augier, still quite a young man, had only attained a second or third place in that school of common sense which was first and foremost a protest against Romanticism. A protest, be it observed, a trifle blind and narrow-minded, since in Hugo's case it confounded the great lyrical poet with the half-developed dramatist. People had forgotten that the Romanticism which appealed *urbi et orbi* in the preface to "Cromwell" was but the successor of an earlier Romanticism, which had found expression in Stendhal's pamphlet, *Racine and Shakespeare.* The world seemed ignorant of the fact that before becoming Christian and Gothic, the Romanticists had proposed to return to historical truth and local colour, and above all to psychological analysis. They were but seeking to hand on the tradition of Arnaud, Picard, Andrieux, the Duvals, Soumet, Casimir Delavigne, and the whole classical group of the Restoration. It was no literary revolution, merely a reaction, a reversion. Like the emigrants of 1815, they had learned nothing and forgotten nothing. Hugo was another Bonaparte: we had escaped from his influence as from a nightmare, and congratulated ourselves that we could so quickly obliterate the last trace of the usurper's passage.

This was a bad beginning. Augier took part in the crusade of mediocrity against genius, and was not above the somewhat mean and petty sentiments which animated his companions. As I have just said, he was not the first amongst them; even fifteen years afterwards people were still asking whether François Ponsard, the author of *Lucrèce* and the *Lion Amoureux*, was not the greater man of the two. Augier was no stranger to all the faults of the common-sense school. He wrote in a style which had borrowed its false air of antiquity from the older comic writers. To suppose yourself to belong to the " grand siècle," because you season your dialogue with " Vous vous moquez," " j'enrage," " la peste soit du fat," and other such phrases borrowed from Molière, Regnard, and Marivaux, is in itself one of the most innocent of literary fads. Unfortunately for Augier the archaic character of his phraseology was not in keeping with the modernity of his sentiment. At no time in his life had he the faintest glimmering of the historical sense; there is no more Hellenism about his *Ciguë* than there is Latinity in his *Joueur de Flûte.* He had clearly no other reason for writing these plays than the wish to protest, with Ponsard, against the German and mediæval tendencies of the opposite school by stamping his work with a Grecian temple in opposition to a Gothic cathedral. The scene of *Diane* is laid in the age of Richelieu, but it bears no mark of its date except its costumes and a few political allusions. Shorn of its powder and patches, we should forget that the action of *Philiberte* takes place in the eighteenth century. Augier could not even carry his imagination back fifteen years to a time which he knew perfectly well. Compare the *Effrontés* with the *Fils de Giboyer*, and you will see that there appears to be no difference between 1845 and 1858, between the period of his youthful efforts and the society in which his riper years had been spent. Still, lack of the historic sense is a fault which can be remedied by letting the past alone and choosing a subject from one's own immediate surroundings. It is a graver error to surround the *bourgeois* mind and *bourgeois* society with a poetic halo altogether out of keeping. Augier shared this mania, which was common to all his friends, and carried it further that any of them. The party of the Left Centre, the "happy mean" of French opinion, imposed this condition upon the authors of the common-sense school if they wished to be acknowledged as its favourite interpreters. Snobbishness is well known to adopt all sorts of disguises. When a tradesman had grown rich and wanted his portrait painted he liked to see a thoughtful, imperious figure, with one hand thrust into his waistcoat and the other behind his back in the traditional attitude of Napoleon. Of course Dupont and Durant were charmed to hear themselves declaiming verses like an Agamemnon, a Mithridates, or an Orosmane. The *vers aux bourgeois* were part of the spoils of '89, and, like all other spoils, the middle class intended to keep a firm grip upon them. From 1845 to 1860 they were given their fill of poetry.

Was Augier a poet? Certainly not; but hidden away in the furthest and most ideal recess of his nature lurked a secret spring of song. A few couplets there are of his, half-tender, half-sad, which I can never hear without a little thrill of pleasure. Now and again his coarser humour borrowed the changing hues of De Musset's capricious fancy; in one of those hours he composed *L'Aventurière.* Played to empty benches during the most troublous days of 1848, this charming comedy, retouched by the author, has contrived to survive. It has become, in a sense, classic, and deservedly so. You can still see the *bourgeois* and the Bohemians of the time, but they take the stage in such gallant guise that what they have to say genuinely deserves to be said in verse.

I cannot conscientiously mete out the same praise to *Gabrielle* or to *La Jeunesse,* which, nevertheless, were great successes at the time, and still command traditional respect. They are antiquated both in form and in substance.

There are perhaps a dozen lines of real poetry in *La Cigüe,* as many in *Philiberte,* and a hundred or perhaps more in *L'Aventurière.* As to *La Jeunesse,* prose itself could hardly be more prosaic. Certainly there is a lower depth still, for we have *Le Fruit Défendu* and *La Considéra-tion;* but Augier had already struck a sufficiently false note when he justified the existence of Camille Doucet. At all costs the *bourgeoisie* had to be made poetical, but the only result was to make poetry *bourgeois* and to kill it in the process. The idea of making verses trip from the tongues of Dupont and Durant had perforce to be abandoned.

Although the movement suffered shipwreck in this quarter, it succeeded elsewhere and developed beyond all expectation. I said just now that it was a struggle between mediocrity and genius: the victory lay with mediocrity. Nor is this a matter either for surprise or for regret. Genius was in the wrong, and it was the mediocre people who were clinging most closely to our traditions, and who had the clearest conception of the future towards which thought in France was tending. France is a nation of Realists; she was born Realist, pre-destined thereto by some freak of atavism, since in her there lives again the genius of the Latin people.   Realism inspired her *fabliaux* and romances in the Middle Ages; a Realist she remained from century to century with her Montaigne, her Bossuet, her Voltaire, her Mérimée; she is a Realist in religion and in poetry, she carries her Realism into the very domain of the ideal, for to her Realism is a mode of existence rather than a method of thought. Though diverted at times from this path, she returns to it.   After 1850 the French mind made a vigorous and universal effort to grasp the living reality in everything, and to escape from the bondage of symbols and abstractions. Many things combined to favour such an effort. There was first the bankruptcy of the opposite party, and then the great silence which had fallen on politics.   "L'Empire, c'est la paix!" said Napoleon III. in a famous speech : and in spite of a few wars, too distant or too quickly over to disturb the active life of the nation, I am inclined to hold that, after all, the saying proved true. At all events it was so for the literary world. As I had often occasion to notice, no sovereign has ever had more respect for talent.   Augier had cause to know this. When an unintelligent Minister wanted to stop the *Fils de Giboyer*, the Emperor was appealed to by the author; he annulled the censor's decision, and Giboyer said his say. Louis XIV. had, in like manner, protected the author of *Tartufe;* Augier recalled the fact in his preface, and it was thought that the comparison was in itself the highest compliment which gratitude could suggest.

Ah! those were glorious days. The critics who belittle them, or who reproach the men of the time with their thirst for pleasure, forget to add that the thirst for knowledge was no whit less keen. Both, indeed, spring fundamentally from one and the same mental condition, which produces different effects according to the nobility or vulgarity of men's minds. What efforts were made! What victories were won! Renan gave back to history the immense tracts which theology had wrested from it, Sainte-Beuve was preparing the road for Taine, whose mission it was to raise criticism into a system, and to make it the keystone of all knowledge, the science of all sciences. Pasteur was building up his apparatus in that humble laboratory in the Rue d'Ulm whence so many discoveries were destined to issue. A boundless enthusiasm was abroad, a limitless confidence. It seemed as if science would prove all-powerful, would solve every question, answer every need, satisfy every yearning after knowledge, realise every dream of humanity. Poetry could do nothing but abdicate, doubly suspect as it must perforce confess itself, for it had not only grovelled in the depths of Classicism, but had lost its way in endeavouring to follow the flight of the Romanticists. It took refuge in small gatherings of the faithful, where it could serve as a consolation to the discontented, and an intellectual exercise to those *virtuosi* who were to be nicknamed the Parnassiens. The novel, on the other hand, was attacking the most important questions and invading every region of existence. Instead of sending verses home from the land of his exile, Victor Hugo issued a novel in eight volumes. Every year the *Revue des Deux Mondes* gave its readers a new work by George Sand. Whilst humourists of the second rank, such as Mürger and Champfleury, were describing remote corners of the provinces or the manners of the Quartier Latin, Gustave Flaubert was laboriously composing the pages of *Madame Bovary*. Realism was supreme on the stage, but only that modified form of Realism which does not seek to rob the drama of its twofold function as a work of art and an instrument of moral education. From 1852 onwards Alexandre Dumas brilliantly justified his claim to stand side by side with Augier. Towards the close of the first decade of the Empire, *Monsieur Garat*, the *Prés St. Gervais*, and the *Pattes de Mouche* had illustrated Victorien Sardou's astonishing power of manipulating a dramatic intrigue. The fierce war which Théodore Barrière was waging against vice and stupidity in the *Filles de Marbre* and the *Faux Bonshommes*, and even in the *Jocrisses de l'Amour*, seemed to herald the rise of a new but an ill-tempered Molière. Henri Meilhac, Parisian first and Frenchman second, was sketching the manners of studio and smoking-room with his admirable lightness of touch, and immortalising those little peculiarities of speech and sentiment which are but the passing fashion of a day.

Labiche, with his more solid and sober gifts, was unwittingly raising farce to the level of comedy by drawing pictures of *bourgeois* life as true and genial as they are genuinely comic. Octave Feuillet was transferring the heroes and heroines of his novels to the stage, and with them the chivalrous dream of moral refinement, the nervous and exquisite melancholy, belonging to his innermost nature. However enamoured a society may be of realistic effects, in its moments of reaction it will seek such outlets of emotion as inevitably as a happy woman will indulge in occasional outbursts of tears. For two hundred nights an audience of journalists, financiers, *cocodettes*, and even *cocottes* wept over the misfortunes of the *Jeune Homme Pauvre*.

But let me leave Octave Feuillet to his novels, Labiche to his vaudevilles, and Meilhac to the brilliant fantasies or the parodies which he has made so peculiarly his own ; as for poor Barrière, he fell by the road halfway up the hill of glory. Victorien Sardou is, I think, so well known in England, where numbers of his pieces have been successfully adapted, that I may leave him out of this study. I acknowledge that he mastered his trade more completely than any other dramatist, and that if I wanted to point out the excellences of that form of dramatic art in which Scribe was a past master, Victorien Sardou must be accorded the foremost place. But I take a different point of view. The theatre only interests me in so far as it is related to the history of ideas and sentiments. I have nothing to learn from M. Victorien Sardou, nor will my grandchildren have much, as to the thoughts and feelings of the men and women of our time. He is not a representative writer. In Sardou I only find Scribe, whereas in Augier and Dumas, over and above Augier and Dumas I find a whole epoch, a society, and a habit of thought which lasted in France for thirty years.

I was at school (in 1860) when I first saw Augier and Dumas. Augier, with his bright brown eyes and massive brow, created an impression of strength and solidity. The leading feature of his face was the large hooked nose, which the Romans regarded as a sign of sarcastic humour. What struck me most in Alexandre

Dumas *fils*, was the discovery that he was both
so like and so unlike his father. How could
that half-blanched negro, with puffed-out over-
hanging cheeks, have produced the fine gentleman, whose every point proclaimed the man
beloved of women? Yet the features were the
same, though emphasized, refined, and idealised.
When a stranger was presented to him, he
looked searchingly, almost sternly, at him, his
face softening or darkening according to the impression received. He seemed a man whose
judgments were sudden and instinctive, prompted
by impulse or antipathy; and his plays, like his
prefaces, bore traces of his quick sensibility.
When I met him again, fifteen years later, at
the baths in the mountains of Auvergne, his
curly hair had turned grey, his complexion had
grown muddy and bilious, and the expression of
his blue eyes alternated between fierce disdain
and quiet pity. The author of the *Demi-Monde*
had given place to the author of the *Femme de
Claude.* Augier I never saw again, except on
a certain winter night, when I stood before
his bust in the Place de l'Odéon. A ray of

moonlight shivered across his forehead, and there was a smile on his lips, as if he had just lighted upon the *mot* which closes *Le Gendre de M. Poirier.*

As writers for the stage these two men introduced no innovations. They accepted, without dispute or modification, the form and the principles of dramatic architecture adopted by Scribe. It was a strange enough mixture when one comes to think of it, a sort of *pot-pourri* of every known style. The older critics distinguished three kinds of comedy, the comedy of character, the comedy of manners, and the comedy of intrigue, instanced as it might be in *L'Avare, Les Fâcheux,* and *Les Fourberies de Scapin.* You will find this distinction constantly made use of by Désiré Nisard in his *Histoire de la Littérature Française,* which in 1860 was still the law and the prophets. Scribe had amalgamated these three forms of comedy with the *bourgeois* drama invented by Diderot, and made an actual reality by Sedaine. The first act was to be given up to explanation, with a final scene in which the action opened; then after oscillating between good and evil fortune, like a game of chess in which the chances are evenly balanced, the fourth act—as a rule the *Acte du Bal*—crowded the stage with supers and culminated in some scandal, a duel, or a similar event in prospect. The fifth act put everything straight, and ended with a proper distribution of rewards and punishments. The first act was invariably bright; during the succeeding acts the action passed from comedy to drama by imperceptible gradations, and the final note was a note of tender, or playful, serenity, a feeling of having had a lucky escape—something like the famous verdict: *Not guilty, but don't do it again.* It was left to psychology and social satire to clothe the bones and muscles of the play with living flesh, and to convert it into a unity. If the comedy of manners and the dramatic intrigue fell apart, the play had failed; if the two elements were perfectly fused, the play was a good one. There was no other criterion.

It would convey an incomplete idea of the somewhat trivial complexities of this method if I omitted to mention that each act had to contain at least one great scene, composed according to certain fixed rules. The play arose out of the development of one or more characters acting upon each other, the scene out of the development of a situation. The scene, like the play itself, had its working up, its catastrophe, and its conclusion; it was, as it were, a complete and separate creation within another creation, a work of art included in another work of art, just like those delicate lace-like ivory cups that Chinese sculptors carve and fit one within another in a diminishing series.

Even that is not all, for there is the parallel intrigue, which Scribe had borrowed from the Romantic drama, or, if you prefer it, the Shakesperian drama, and adapted to his own purposes. This second intrigue, sad if the first was gay, or gay if the first was sad, might recall the first by way of refutation or parody, contrast or reflection; it might transpose it into another key, or it might take a directly contrary line. The two parallel intrigues began by being perfectly distinct, and ended by converging and contributing each their share to the dénouement.   If all the threads were not gathered up, the critics counted the author a novice ignorant of his trade, and sent him back to study good models.

Augier and Dumas had nothing to urge against such an arrangement. This form suited them as well as any other for conveying their ideas. Besides, they saw one thing clearly which escapes our younger writers for the stage, namely, that intrigue is not only indispensable to the spectator's amusement, but that it is of the very essence of psychological development. Characters cannot be studied in repose like insects under a microscope. They have not even arrived at self-consciousness, they might almost be said to have only a provisional, potential existence, until the moment when they come into contact and into conflict with events or with other characters. I will take a striking example. The drama of the French Revolution threw into relief thousands of existences which, without it, would have passed into nothingness and oblivion. If there had been no revolution, Collot d'Herbois would have remained a mere strolling player; Marat a veterinary surgeon ; Legendre a butcher ; Chabot a Capuchin friar ; Hoche a sergeant of the guard; Fouché would have been whipping the little scholars of the Oratorians; Talleyrand reciting the Mass without a particle of faith in it; Robespierre and Carnot, the one a third-rate lawyer and the other an obscure captain, would have gone on exchanging trivial verses in the Academy of the Rosati; Bonaparte, put on half-pay because of his evil reputation, would have died of fever in a corner of his native island, remembered only as a troublesome neighbour, a somewhat undisciplined officer, and a rather ridiculous author. But the drama in which their lot was cast revealed to us their power for good or evil. So, too, with an imaginary drama. As long as a human being has been neither loved, betrayed, nor given cause for jealousy, as long as he has never been called to be the ruin or the salvation of other human beings, to fall or to retrieve a fall, to pardon or to take vengeance, it is useless to study him, he is nothing but a blank page.

Augier and Dumas were willing, therefore, to accept Scribe's conception of dramatic form. Superficially their plays do not differ sensibly from his, but what is primary with them was only accessory with him, and what he employed as means to an end became with them an end in itself. Scribe gave us studies of character and pictures of manners for the sake of writing plays; Augier and Dumas wrote plays for the sake of studying character and painting manners. Thence it was but a step to what we call in modern parlance the "problem play." Augier never took the step; he never ventured beyond political and social satire. A problem implies a paradox. The defence of conjugal love, for example, is perfectly simple; but the redemption of the courtesan brings the "problem" straightway to the fore. Hence the world imagined a problem in Dumas' very first piece *La Dame aux Camélias*, wherein he was really only giving vent to his youthful ardour in a storm of passion and tears. This unjust accusation proved itself a just presentiment, and taught Dumas his vocation. What he had been wrongfully accused of doing in the *Dame aux Camélias*, he did of set purpose, and in a burst of enthusiasm, in the *Demi-Monde*, the *Question d'Argent*, the *Père Prodigue*, the *Fils Naturel*, above all in the *Idées de Madame Aubray* and the plays which followed.

Into this ready-made mould, which I have described, and with hardly any alteration, Augier and Dumas poured their wit and their philosophy. Their wit first and foremost, for both were amply dowered with it. Augier's was the merrier; Dumas' the more original and suggestive. The former was an adept in the art of making epigrams, whilst the latter had a weakness for tirades. A whole school of actors and actresses arose with a talent for the effective delivery of an epigram or a tirade. I don't mean to say that the French artists of the time had no other merit; many had completely mastered the art of creating a character, and some of their creations have remained traditions of the stage. When they had lighted upon the character, for which their physical endowments rendered them most fitted, they repeated it in play after play, made the most complete study of it, and brought it to a veritable pitch of perfection. Such a part was created by Paulin Ménier at the Boulevard, in his Père Martin, his Escamoteur, and his Chopart in the *Courrier de Lyon*. Provost, of the Théâtre Français, and Geoffroy, of the Palais Royal, did the same for different types of the species *bour-geois*. There was Samson, again, in the Marquis de la Seiglière and all similar parts, and Lafont, of the Gymnase, with his irresistibly graceful impersonation of an aged Don Juan. From all these the public asked nothing better than that they should go on as they were. And I reserved a special place in my gallery of remembrance for Lafontaine, the actor who most deeply stirred my youthful enthusiasm. I can still see his high forehead shining with intelligence, his expressive eyes, his fascinating kindly smile. He could be both excellent and execrable in one and the same part, and was the only actor whom I ever saw vary his effects and abandon himself to inspiration when actually on the stage.

But the artists of those days were first and foremost astonishing elocutionists. One went to the Vaudeville simply to hear Fargueil in the *Mariage d'Olympe* exclaim, "J'aurais le maximum," with an accent which brought a shuddering recollection of the Old Bailey. In the *Effrontés* one waited for Provost and his "Que voulez-vous? J'aime la gloire," or Madame

Plessy's "Mais bats-moi donc," or Samson's "De mon temps, on avait Dieu," just as a little later the world crowded to hear Tamberlik's high C. These *mots* came thick and fast throughout the dialogue, and the audience never wearied of them. They were repeated in the press and in society, and they made the success of the piece.

Even after making almost all their characters brilliant, and putting epigrams into the mouths of absolute imbeciles, the authors were far from having exhausted their resources. It became the custom to introduce a character who had nothing to do but to make brilliant comments, and whose task it was to explain everything and to pass judgment upon everything in the half-serious fashion of a reviewer. But was this character really invented by Augier or Dumas? Was it not a revival in another form of Molière's Ariste, the light sarcastic *blagueur* replacing the gentle pedant of the older comedies? And to go back still further, are not both reminiscences of the Chorus of antiquity?

Dumas employs this device with even greater freedom than Augier. The drama seems at first sight the most impersonal of all forms of literary art: the showman's place is to remain hidden behind his puppets. But Dumas could not so efface himself and relinquish his own personality, and for my own part I rejoice in his incapacity, for I can no longer conceal the fact that what I love best in his plays is just himself. What do I care if he did violate the rules of his art? I hate your impassive people; I like to feel a heart beating behind novel or drama, more especially such a noble heart. Consequently—and this is a cardinal point—Dumas threw his whole heart and soul, his very self, into his work. He is on the stage in the person of Olivier de Jalin (*Demi-Monde*), or Ryons (*L'Ami des Femmes*), or Rémonin (*L'Etrangère*), or ten other characters, observing, directing, and criticising his own play, except where the critic happens to be merged in the lover. And this is why he loses himself in his work, whilst Augier contrives to remain apart. Augier did no more than · enshrine his conception of life in his plays; Dumas poured into them his very life itself.

Augier's dramatic work might be summed up

as a crusade against wealth and a defence of marriage. The social question, as it was then understood, was very simple. What *modus vivendi* could be established between the aristocracy of finance and the aristocracy of birth? What place could be found for the nobility in modern society? Clearly they might become soldiers or agriculturalists, or even, at a pinch, sons-in-law, if due precaution were exercised. Which side does the author really espouse? I leave *Le Gendre de M. Poirier* out of account, because there is something of Jules Sandeau in that play, and Jules Sandeau was always a little tainted with a sort of belated royalism. But even in the other plays it looks rather as if Augier were disposed to give the marquises the finest parts. Still, like a clever man who tries to propitiate every section of the public, he always placed a type alongside of his antitype, virtue by the side of vice, Verdelet, the modest, sober *bourgeois*, beside Poirier, the *bourgeois* eaten up with vanity, just as he contrasts the Duc de Montmayran, who dons a volunteer's helmet and goes off to the African wars, with the Marquis de Presle, who runs riot with his wife's dowry; or again, Sergines the estimable journalist, with Vernouillet, who is utterly unscrupulous. Such skilful devices serve to disarm criticism, but serve also to confuse the moral. Still, it does not need any very long process of reflection to discover the author's intention. *Bourgeois* at heart, he can only castigate the *bourgeoisie* somewhat after the method of Sancho Panza when undergoing his self-inflicted discipline. He wills not the death of the sinner, but rather that he should be converted and live. He believed in the future of the middle classes, and had no desire, like so many modern reformers, to deprive them of riches and power, but merely to cure them of certain ugly faults, the faults of *parvenus,* which he took upon himself to correct. Let them learn to place honour above money, to recognise that devotion and self-sacrifice are the price that must be paid for greatness and power. He is so sure that the middle-class ideal will rise from generation to generation that he does not hesitate to make children teach their parents. It is not enough for young Charier that his father makes full retribution to all the creditors belonging to an old and forgotten bankruptcy; he must immolate himself upon the altar of fate, and make atonement for the luxuries and pleasures to which he thinks he had no right, by embracing the hardships of a soldier's life. And how does Mdlle. Poirier win back her faithless scion of nobility? By three acts of disinterestedness, which might be not unfairly called three acts of folly; by paying debts which are not really due, by tearing up a letter which might prove a useful weapon in a law court, and by sending her husband to fight a duel, the very cause of which is an offence against herself. All this is, of course, exaggerated, but, like all his contemporaries, Augier believed firmly that on the stage honesty must assume heroic proportions, and the moral be writ so large that it could be read from every part of the house. Actors of antiquity mounted on stilts and spoke through speaking trumpets; Augier's moral philosophy followed their example.

Augier had been a student at the Collège Henri IV., where the Orleans Princes were among his companions. In this ancient and famous institution he had imbibed the teachings of the philosophy known as eclecticism, which Victor Cousin was then forcing upon the university with all the authority of a dictator. This philosophy, borrowing as it did from Plato and Leibnitz, Descartes and Kant, without disdaining the rather unimaginative psychology of the worthy Reid and his successors, steadfastly maintained the existence of a personal God distinct from the natural order which He created and which He preserves, the spiritual character of the soul and its immortality, the theory of innate ideas, of free-will and responsibility, the double catalogue of works of mercy and justice, the rewards and punishments of a future life. It allowed dogma to shroud itself in a veil of possibility, and got on very well without it; it went so far as to give a provisional denial to the theories of miracles, and contrasted natural religion with theology. This is the philosophy which I feel throughout Augier's work.

Consequently he looked upon life as a desirable thing, and thence arose his respect for the exalted *rôle* of the mother. Himself the best of sons, he

has drawn a sweet and touching picture of mater-
nity in his Maman Guérin, whose instinct discerns
and baffles every rascally device. Motherhood,
even when illegitimate, sanctifies, in his eyes,
every woman who accepts its burdens; witness
Madame Bernard in the *Fourchambault.* But it
was the defence of marriage which inspired him
more than anything else. His very first play
disclosed his sentiments on this point. In
ancient Athens itself, the very spot where the
courtesan was the intellectual companion of man,
and a married woman was nothing more than a
servant and a machine for bearing children, he
laid the scene of a play which glorified married
life and the one exclusive bond of love that
unites the man for ever to one woman and the
woman to one man. He was not content with
fidelity after marriage: he would have a young
man keep faith beforehand with her who was as
yet unknown to him, but who, on her side, was
guarding for him alone the innocent treasure of
her thoughts. Listen to the despairing regrets
of the man who lacked foresight and patience,
and had failed to keep his heart pure, as be-

seemed the temple, which the divine guest was to enter :

> "Ah ! maudite à jamais soit la première femme,
> Qui de ce droit chemin a détourné mon âme !
> Maudit soit le premier baiser qui m'a séduit !
> Maudit tout ce qui m'a loin du bonheur conduit !"

Thus Fabrice in *L'Aventurière*, and it is no idle curse. "La femme sans pudeur," it is said in another play, "n'est pas plus une femme que l'homme sans courage n'est un homme." Crush her underfoot without mercy as you would a snake. This is what the old Marquis does in the *Mariage d'Olympe*, it is what Fabrice comes near to doing in *L'Aventurière*, and it is the idea suggested to the spectator's mind by the dénouement of the *Lionnes Pauvres*. And who is it that speaks in this key and delivers these merciless sentences ? Instead of a French dramatist of the Second Empire, you might imagine the speaker a Stubbes, a Stephen Gosson, a Prynne, or some voice still more remote, belonging to those fierce primitive societies where adultery was punished with death. Yet side by side with these outbursts of severity there breathes a strange tenderness for the vagabond, the ill-regulated, and the irresponsible, whose failures are due to weakness, ignorance, or frivolity. Forgiveness is never far off, and it needs but a tear to obtain it. Herein Augier parts company with the Puritans only to draw closer to the Gospel.

The author of *L'Aventurière* is no frigid professor of morals, but a passionate lover of virtue. You find the same passion in Dumas, but his genius tends to pessimism; enthusiasm for good becomes a fierce hatred of evil. And, in his eyes, the evil-doer is not he who violates the law, but he who inflicts suffering upon a loving heart. Woman fills the whole stage in his theatre, just as she fills his thoughts and his whole life. Man plays only a secondary part; he is a satellite revolving round the principal luminary. By his conduct towards woman he must stand or fall; but by what rule shall she be judged? Let her only love much and all her sins shall be forgiven her by Dumas. All virtue comes to her through love, or rather, love in her constitutes virtue. "Il faut aimer," says Madame Aubray, "n'importe qui, n'importe quoi, n'importe comment, pourvu qu'on aime ! " The chief test of a woman's sincerity is found in her devotion to her child, whether this child be born in wedlock or in lawless love. And as Madame Aubray says again in this play—which is so poor a play and so admirable a book—" Jusqu'à ce qu'elle soit mère, la femme peut errer; elle peut ignorer où réside le véritable amour et le chercher à tort et à travers. A partir de l'heure où elle a un enfant, elle sait à quoi s'en tenir. Si elle se soustrait à ce devoir, c'est qu'elle est décidément sans cœur." Against a final judgment like this there can hardly be any appeal; but wait a moment—here is a sentence which opens the door to the fullest indulgence. " Il n'y a pas de méchants, pas de coupables, pas d'ingrats; il n'y a que des malades, des aveugles et des fous."

Madame Aubray goes beyond Dumas. If we want to get his point of view, we must seek it in Olivier de Jalin and M. de Ryons. The latter christens himself " L'Ami des Femmes "; the former is their enemy. Both these characters are to be found in Dumas' own nature. With

Ryons he holds out his hand to the woman who has not yet fallen though she is trembling on the brink, or to the woman already fallen but striving to retrieve her fall. For the other sort of woman, the " fille " who is a courtesan by birth and by instinct, in the person of Olivier de Jalin he shows no sort of chivalry or consideration; he crushes her even more brutally than Augier. If need be the judge will turn executioner. "Tue-la!" is the conclusion of the famous pamphlet, and it is also the dénouement of the *Femme de Claude*. If he does not kill her, he kills her accomplice; if he spares both, he implants in our souls so bitter a disgust for feminine prostitution and masculine baseness that the effect is far greater than the spectacle of the most terrible vengeance could ever have produced. Hitherto the sort of morality which is a matter of feeling rather than of actual fact has hardly been understood in England. I took occasion to mention this àpropos of Sydney Grundy's plays, to which Puritans take so much exception, although to my mind they are eminently healthy and invigorating. On the other hand, they applauded Robertson's dénouements, although Robertson never suggested any rule of conduct, unless it were a stupid one, such as that the poor are of more moral worth than the rich. Nevertheless, he took good care to endow his heroes with this world's goods in the closing scene, which deprived his precept of all its value. If you read *La Princesse Georges* your whole soul will revolt against its dénouement, and I myself have great difficulty in reconciling my mind to it. The greatest sinner goes unpunished; the faithless husband is delivered from an infamous mistress, and has but to step back again across the threshold of conjugal felicity; the deceived husband is about to be led away to prison as a murderer; the betrayed wife may indeed forgive, but she will suffer all her life; young Fondette gives his life as the price of his service in the courts of love. He has a mother, and that mother, whom I have never seen and do not know, but who interests me and wins my love solely because she is a mother who has lost her child, will suffer keenly enough to make me detest this ending to the play. And that half-comic, half-tragic figure of Cigneroi, in the *Visite de Noces*, whose love for his former mistress is re-awakened by imagining the different ways in which she may have betrayed him, and whom Dumas sends home again with his pretty sleeping baby and his smiling and innocent young wife, at the end of that short act which contains so many revelations as to the ugly depths of our moral nature. What does all this matter? Why need we trouble ourselves about the seeming injustice of fate, if only justice sits enthroned within, if our minds are set in the right direction, if we share the author's vigorous and laudable indignation against these people and all their works? It is the righteous indignation of saints and philosophers, it represents all that is best in us; it is the salt of the earth, the leaven of sudden heroism, and is it not thereby also the inspirer of patient virtue?

I have recognised Dumas in Olivier de Jalin and de Ryons, and I find him also in the person of Rémonin in *L'Etrangère*. The man is always the same, never weary of analysing and expounding the female heart. He sets forth his classification in the first act, and begins all over again in the second; if there were ten acts we should have ten lectures by Rémonin. De Jalin and de Ryons were men of the world: Rémonin is a *savant.* "L'Amour, c'est de la physique; le mariage, c'est de la chimie." Here comes in the famous "theory of *vibrions.*" Shall I confess that I rather misdoubt Dumas' physics and chemistry? They seem to me more curious than exact, more striking than profound. But the change indicates an important fact—the fact that since the author's youth the world had advanced and that psychology was on the high road to becoming a science.

I doubt whether there could be a great man nowadays who was not a bit of an Anarchist. Alexandre Dumas treated our upper classes with the contempt that they deserve; he abuses them in the style of Rousseau and Tolstoi. "Notre fortune n'est pas à nous," says Madame Aubray's son. "A qui donc est-elle? A tous ceux qui en ont besoin." So much for property; as for the institution of marriage, Dumas might be said to have attacked it, but only for the same good reasons which led Augier to defend it. He wished to see divorce established that marriage might be strengthened and purified; he reached his goal, but it has proved only a halting-place. In short, all the great problems that occupy our minds and fill them with feverish anxiety are to be found in the writings of the last twenty years of his life. I should add that although, like his contemporary, he seeks to base the moral law upon natural sentiments, he keeps the higher sanction in reserve.

The defeat of 1870 left an open wound ever bleeding in the hearts of the two dramatists. Augier in *Jean de Thommeray* gives us an aristocratic young libertine for whom the *place* of the Palais Royal becomes the way to Damascus. The sight of his father passing by at the head of a regiment of volunteers works his instant conversion: he throws himself into the ranks and demands a musket amidst cries of "Vive la France." How far preferable to this theatrical scene is the simple exhortation addressed by Claude to his disciple in the silence of his laboratory: "Homme de vingt ans, qui as peut-être encore quarante ans à vivre, que viens-tu me parler de chagrins d'amour? C'était bon autrefois. Et ton Dieu qu'il te faut retrouver? Et ta conscience qu'il te faut établir? Et ta patrie qu'il te faut refaire?" Solemn words, full of a sublime severity: I pity the Frenchman who can hear or read them unmoved.

These are your light-hearted triflers, your corrupters of youth! Ah! you will love them when you know them, but to know them you must get rid of the censorship, which puts you to bed like children just when grown-up people are beginning to discuss their affairs seriously. And you must also get rid of a certain ill-met race of adapters who disfigure these essentially French plays by Anglicising them instead of giving them to you just as they were written. It is easy to criticise and amend Augier's and Dumas' dramatic system, and to blame their use of wit and epigram, but moralists they are and must remain, and it would not be difficult to show that they share that honour with Barrière, Feuillet, Labiche, and Meilhac himself—yes, even Meilhac. Frenchmen have always had a liking for intro-

spection and for philosophising about their sentiments and passions; by such exercises they have
acquired that quickness and subtlety of mind,
and also that gift of emotion, which have drawn
down upon them the reproach or the envy of
other nations. In their sermons, their novels,
their historical writings, this moralising-tendency
is for ever reappearing. The moralists represent,
in short, the flower of our genius, the very essence
of France. Dumas is one of the greatest, and if
the day ever dawns when his pieces are no longer
played, a volume of his sayings must be placed
on the same shelf with Pascal's Thoughts, with
Montaigne's Essays, and with the Maxims of
Larochefoucauld.

II.

NATURALISM ON THE STAGE.

THAT still numerous body of persons who witnessed the struggle against the Prussians and the tragedies of the Commune must admit, if they are sincere, that they expected to see France emerge from her terrible experiences completely changed. Would she be better or worse ? In any case she would be different; the future would see another nation with other ideas, other manners, and a wholly different conception of literature and art. The soul of the people had been stirred to its very depths, the upheaval had been so complete that nothing could henceforth stand where it stood before. Each individual felt as if he had lost a dearly loved friend; surely, then, the collective existence, which is after all but a combination of separate existences, must be affected by so great a change !

I shared this impression myself. When I

revisited Paris during those days of heavy stupor and angry humiliation which intervened between the two sieges, I could hardly recognise the city. No carriages, no beautiful dresses, not a sign of luxury. Nothing but pale faces, sombre colours, ragged and dirty uniforms, sadness and poverty on every side. Could this be going to last? Were the Athenians to turn Spartans? Should we henceforth be a nation of austere and silent workers, a people with one fixed idea, and a burning contempt for all that it had formerly adored? I was soon to be enlightened. By the autumn of 1871 Paris had already almost regained the aspect with which I had been familiar in the days of the Empire. The sight of it reminded me of that saying of Linnæus, which contains the germ of the whole theory of evolution, "Natura non facit saltus." It is one of those truths, as true as truth itself, upon which the human mind can safely rest, and upon which I base my faith. No, nature does not proceed by leaps and bounds; the crisis of an hour works no greater change in a society than it does in an individual.

Everything, then, appeared to resume its accustomed course, and to be as it was on the eve of the catastrophe. If there was a shade of difference noticeable, it was only a vaguely retrospective and archaic tendency on the part of the ruling class. Old men who had been sulking in corners, some for eighteen years and some for forty, crept out of their retreats to stretch their old limbs and sun themselves in the fresh air of the Place d'Armes, now that Versailles had resumed its supremacy. The Marquis de la Seiglière was again governing France in conjunction with M. Poirier. Worthy M. Poirier! how the world had laughed at his announcement that he would become a peer of France *in* 1848; but the laughter died away when he was created perpetual senator in 1875. All the world knows that this revolution came very near to a restoration. Who knows whether the monarchy would not have been actually re-established, if the descendant of the kings had been willing to drape the banner of Austerlitz round the standard of Ivry and Fontenoy? The fate of literature, under these conditions, could easily have been foreseen; it was like taking up a book again after a passing interruption at the very page and line, nay, the very word where it had been laid down. The war had given birth to an infinity of publications, memoirs, defences, revelations, recriminations, schemes of revenge and patriotic songs. Gradually the torrent of printed matter dried up. In the theatres the same actors went on playing the same pieces—or pieces very like them—before the same audiences, and such talent as rose to the surface was modelled on the pattern that had found favour in the eyes of the preceding epoch.

First the artists. I will take a few names amongst those whose success was most striking. For fifteen years Céline Chaumont, whom people in England will probably remember, held the place on our stage which is now filled by Réjane. I saw her make her début when she was almost a child in *l'Ami des Femmes* at the Gymnase. She was Déjazet's favourite pupil, but she combined the lightness and playfulness of Déjazet's " vieille France " style with that dose of modern realism which her audience demanded. What did she represent? Parisian and feminine *esprit* in its perfection. She had a genius for underlining, but she ended by underlining everything, which is as good as underlining nothing. Her elocution was so studied that she almost made her hearers weary of the art which had delighted Society in the days of the Second Empire. Her theatrical forbears were Dupuis and Daubray— Dupuis the successor of Shakespeare's fools, Daubray the embodiment of geniality. The authors who wrote parts for them, and the public which applauded them, forgot the characters that they were meant to represent; they could see and hear nothing but Dupuis or Daubray. Madame Judic had the same sort of success; the actress was everything, the rôle nothing. To utter enormities, or to commit them with the most ingenuous air in the world, was Madame Judic's speciality; deprive her of that and you robbed the good people of Paris of one of their chief pleasures. In every piece written for her there was one particularly risky situation or costume, some refrain, some *mot*, some gesture, which brought down the house; it was the crowning moment. Smart people timed themselves to arrive for it and went away after it, delighted with the artist and thoroughly pleased with themselves.

Madame Bartet was suddenly revealed to the Parisian world on the first night of *Fromont jeune et Risler aîné*—a play based upon Alphonse Daudet's famous novel. She played Désirée, the little flower-girl with fairylike fingers, whom every one loves except the one man for whose love she craves. It was as imperishable a creation as Desclée's *Froufrou*. Never had the sorrows of love, the pain and sacrifice which it demands of its lowly victims, been represented on the stage with such grace and delicacy. If my memory is to be trusted this was in September, 1876, and for twenty years Madame Bartet has been repeating her impersonation of loving sorrowful resignation, always with the same grace and the same success. When I saw her in *La Loi de l'Homme*, my neighbour in the stalls said to me, "That is not the real Bartet, our own Bartet that we know; for the first time in her life she is angry and in revolt." The phrase only told me what I knew already, that the generation of 1876 judged dramatic ability by precisely the same standards as the preceding generation. Audiences of that day merely asked of an artist to be herself, always herself, under different names. They liked her to assume one invariable attitude, to repeat the same intonations, and never to weary of expressing the same shade of the same sentiment. One single condition they imposed, perfection in this particular mode of expression. It was thus that, according to Victor Hugo, Greek art condemned

"*Les nymphes à la honte et les faunes au rire.*"

Clearly, all this does not apply to exceptional artists such as Coquelin and Sarah Bernhardt, who combine a strikingly original and individual temperament with a rare power of assimilation and metamorphosis. This double gift will assure them lasting supremacy on the stage, whatever changes may occur in the public taste. Nevertheless, just consider how much of Sarah's success—especially in her earlier parts—was due to her eyes, her smile, her woman's charm, the indefinable grace that she brought into all her parts, and that voice, that famous golden voice, which has been belauded to the verge of ridicule, and yet can never be lauded enough. It would be difficult to exaggerate its importance, for it has changed all the modulations of the feminine voice, not only on the stage but in ordinary conversation.

Theatrical tradition remained intact, and every rising talent was forced into the ancient groove. The same names were always on the bills— Dumas, Augier, Labiche, Meilhac, and Gondinet. Towards the end of the decade 1870-1880 two or three Vaudevillistes made their appearance— Hennequin, Paul Ferrier, Bisson. They were adepts in the art of shuffling a woman out of sight, bandying a husband about, driving a mother-in-law into a fury, and making three intrigues revolve round the same personage. They often had as many as five doors to a *salon*, every one of them indispensable to the action of the play. *Le Procès Vauradieux* and *Les Dominos Roses* promised a long lease of life to that class of writers who produced *Le Chapeau de paille d'Italie* and *La Mariée du Mardi Gras.* In the higher kind of comedy one name had made considerable progress, the name of M. Edouard Pailleron.

He was—or rather is, for he is mercifully very much alive still and in full possession of his gifts—a man of the world and a rich man, which caused him to be mistaken for an amateur. His first efforts took the form of those little rhymed nothings that people call " gems," or " pearls," or " miniature masterpieces," without setting the smallest value upon them. But after a series of successes which culminated in 1881 in *Le Monde où l'on s'ennuie*, M. Pailleron won deserved recognition as a dramatic satirist, a *moqueur* of the first rank, a painter as faithful as he was amusing of the absurdities of high life. He stands unrivalled as the delineator of that particular world which is the home of society pedants, where the virus of academic politics pollutes the air, where society harangues and gives lectures or elegant disquisitions, and creates deputies and " immortals " between two cups of tea. If *Le Monde où l'on s'ennuie* ever disappeared from the contemporary stage, which is most unlikely, it would still be a priceless document in the history of manners. No one ever thought of saying that M. Pailleron's work was unreal; on the contrary, he is accused, at any rate in this particular instance, of having been truthful to the verge of indiscretion, if not betrayal. I do not wish to discuss the question. Since M. Pailleron will not have it so, we will not say that Bellac is a portrait; he is certainly not a caricature. To my mind he represents a combination of the Trissotins and the Tartufes of his class and of his age, for the Church has no monopoly of Tartufes. Philosophy and art have their own, and so too have politics and religion. In 1881 philosophical and artistic Tartuferie consisted in professing a vague sort of idealism, and gently titillating the feminine mind with the languid subtleties of a somewhat silken sort of rhetoric. Bellac did this to perfection. There are some phrases in his speech in the second act which his supposed prototype of the Sorbonne might not have been adverse to accept, if he had had the offer of them ; just as Oronte's sonnet might very well have been appropriated by one of the real *précieux* who contributed to the *Guirlande de Julie.* This is the mark of the great satirists, who touch the really high levels of comedy : they, and they only can both chastise and spare their victims, and can heap coals of fire upon an enemy's head by handing him back his weapons.

M. Pailleron's wit and power of observation are entirely modern, but I cannot say as much for his dramatic architecture. In this respect he is not merely the pupil of Dumas and Augier, he traces his descent through Sardou right back to Scribe. In *Le Monde où l'on s'ennuie* the intrigue turns on a letter, lost by somebody, found by everybody, and giving rise to a double misunderstanding. Some people make a mistake about its authorship, and others about its destination. The most trivial incidents which may serve to prolong the imbroglio, or to aggravate it, are strained to their utmost limits, and lead to a never-ending chain of fresh entanglements, stretching from the first scene to the last.

There is the same complication woven out of petty details in *L'Age Ingrat*, and in *Les Faux Ménages*. In *La Souris* one and the same man is adored or courted by four women, and the way in which their love makes them perform strange evolutions round about him recalls a favourite French game for children. In *Cabotins* the action moves on five parallel lines, corresponding to these five questions: 1. Will Grignoux recover his daughter? 2. Will Pierre marry Valentine? 3. Will Pegomas become Deputy? 4. Will Laversac get into the Institute? 5. Will Madame de Laversac be able to keep the friend who has cost her so much? But though M. Pailleron delights us with his wit, his dramatic problems leave us unfortunately quite unmoved. Then why state the problems? What is the good of these laboured *quiproquos* and these theatrical devices which we are unable to believe in? Does even their author believe in them? Is he really convinced, heart and soul, that salvation cannot be attained without explanations and complications, a catastrophe and a dénouement, without working up a situation and introducing parallel intrigues, in short, without all those vaudeville devices leading up to melodramatic scenes ? I fear not. Characters in his plays are made to strike an attitude in two or three tirades, and to fire off a few epigrams like so many projectiles, out of that carefully calculated store with which the author has stuffed his pouch beforehand, and are then allowed to utter the veriest nothings until their creator wants them again for the dénouement. They are like useless puppets, left limp in a corner, with their arms and heads all tumbling about, until the showman picks up the threads again and makes them dance. M. Pailleron is a sincere enough artist when he is drawing his characters, but he becomes artificial as soon as he has to make them act; whereby we see that he belongs to that stage, inevitable in the history of every school, when method has usurped the place of inspiration. Art, like every other form of creed, has become seriously diseased when the priest is even more incredulous than the faithful.

What did it profit Dumas and the admirers of

the "well-constructed" play that they held all
the points of vantage and gained victory upon
victory? They were but Pyrrhic victories after
all, for the forces of naturalism were pursuing
their relentless advance, and threatened speedily
to overtake their opponents. To ignore the
triumph of naturalism in fiction would at this
time of day be merely childish. For a long
time it was scouted and repudiated, confined,'in
fact, to a narrow circle of doubtful repute. Too
fine-drawn to please the multitude, it was too
brutal for the fastidious. According to the older
critics it could hardly so much as claim to have
roused curiosity or occasioned scandal; even
that poor sort of success was denied to it. Those
incomparable artists, the brothers Goncourt,
gained nothing but a dubious notoriety; Flaubert could only point to one really popular
book, *Madame Bovary*. The world laughed at
Salammbo, and shrugged its shoulders at *L'Education Sentimentale*. Even the first few volumes
of the *Rougon-Macquart* series failed to bring
their author to the front. Towards 1876, however, fashion began to play a part in the matter;

then the question became a burning one and the great battle began. The unprecedented success of *L'Assommoir*, *Nana*, and *Germinal* had its counterpart in the similar and certainly equal success of *Fromont et Risler*, *Le Nabab*, *Les Rois en Exil*, and *Numa Roumestan*. Daudet, when all is said and done, remains Daudet—a poet, an artist, a dreamer, a favoured child of those lands which the sun kisses, where every sound is music and every landscape a picture, where observation is a weariness and invention a delight. Nevertheless many of his pages, and those not the least fine, might be claimed by the naturalists. His contribution to the success of the school was quite as great as that of its chief —nay, perhaps, even greater. Still the world went back to Flaubert and the Goncourts to find the real originators of the movement; however much they had been misconstrued, they were its veritable masters, and yet even Flaubert and the Goncourts counted Stendhal as their progenitor. Poor Stendhal! In 1866 I saw a great heap of manuscript scrawled over in his picturesque handwriting lying neglected in a

corner of the library at Grenoble. These manuscripts, which three generations had despised,
have been religiously collected, page by page,
and given at length to the public.. It is a
striking fact, this resurrection of a much-mis-
understood genius, at the very date which he
had himself assigned to his posthumous fame.

It would not be difficult to show that, three or
four times before in our intellectual history, we
had passed by a natural affinity through a phase
of naturalism, and that though we have left it
behind we shall assuredly return to it. Again,
by converting the *Rougon-Macquart* series into a
weapon against the fallen *régime*, M. Zola enlisted
existing political passions upon his side. Doubtless the Empire had fallen, but imperial society
still survived; both in the Chamber and in the
salons its representatives were making common
cause with returned wanderers from Frohsdorff
and Twickenham. Their final defeat following
upon the sixteenth of May, the retreat of
Marshal MacMahon and Jules Ferry's anti-
clerical campaign coincided with the triumph of
Zola and Daudet. It was more than a mere

coincidence. The author of the *Rougon-Macquart* took care to give his work a democratic character in harmony with the new demands. He was no longer satisfied with idealising the working classes by introducing a few members of the proletariat, and then towards the final pages either raising them to the ranks of the *bourgeoisie,* or making them unnaturally happy in their virtuous poverty after the cunning fashion which had found favour in middle-class literature. It was no longer a question of painting the ideal poor, but the real poor in all their misery, their passion, and their strength. "My book," said the Master of Médan, speaking of *L'Assommoir,* "is the first that really smacks of the people." It was the bible of the *nouvelles couches.*

But what about the fastidious? Were they holding their noses all this time? There are no really fastidious people left, only a set of literary snobs, greedy for subtle and rare sensations. When the first shock is past, they are quite ready and willing to wallow in the mire. They vilified M. Zola, but they bought him. They put him on the index, but only after they had read him. Then they murmured, more to excuse themselves than to do honour to him, "After all, he is a great artist!"

Now Naturalism was applying M. Taine's principles and methods to the analysis of modern life, and that with the most unflinching severity. In every detail of its work, as well as in the work as a whole, it laid stress on the complete subjection of the individual to those three fatal forces — heredity, instinct, and environment. When it had found the "master passion" in a character, there it halted, and insisted upon the subordination of all other moral qualities to this leading quality; the characters which it introduced into its novels were, consequently, simple characters, cut all in one piece, incapable of modification, admitting of no transformation, but working out their development to the bitter end. In such a literature morality counts for nothing and art for very little.

There was not much gaiety about it. George Sand, who belonged to an earlier epoch, confesses that for several days after reading *Jack* she could not so much as hold a pen. For my own part I have never got to the end of one of M. Zola's novels without experiencing a horrible crushing sense of suffocation, as if I were being buried alive and the earth was pressing upon my mouth. No, there was no gaiety about it, but this very fact gave the naturalists their opportunity. France was sad. In the first place defeat had made us gloomy and anxious, and then we had lost the " soft pillow " of the faith that for centuries had lulled our infant slumbers; no sooner had we lost it than we began to look back to it with yearning regret and to extol its soothing power. As to science, it was not keeping the promises which after all it had never made, but which we in our madness had promised ourselves in its name. As the Latin poet has said—

> " Os homini sublime dedit, cœlumque tueri
>   Jussit."

And as we pursued our way within narrow limits and under a gloomy and lowering sky, we could but bow our heads and fix our eyes on the ground. Why look up to heaven if it were empty ? Schopenhauer, from the darkness of his

German grave and the obscurity of his still more German books, held out a hand to the author of *Germinal;* pessimism, whose mission it always is in the long run to bring so many minds back to mysticism, was for the moment lending a helping hand to the fortunes of Naturalism.

One question presented itself for solution. Naturalism had overrun the whole field of fiction; would it also establish itself on the stage?

Augier and Dumas had been borne up at the outset of their career by the tide of realism which issued in Naturalism; but they had been speedily checked in their onward course by the rocks of theatrical conventions, considered inviolable, and also by the fact that their temperament in no wise impelled them in that direction. · Realism in the *mise-en-scène?* Certainly, as much as you please! A real fire on the hearth, a velvet-piled carpet on the floor, the room properly furnished, real champagne and real chickens on the dinner-table—nothing could be better. Dresses which helped the actresses to pose as real women of fashion? By all means. Dialogue a little more like ordinary conversation? Well, perhaps. On this point the two differed. Dumas' dialogue is admirably smooth and natural when he does not happen to be either preaching or theorising, but then he so often is! As for Augier, I know nothing so pleasantly artificial, or so antiquated, from a literary point of view, as the style of *Les Effrontés* and *Le Fils de Giboyer*. Augier has lately been called a realist, but it is not difficult to give the sum-total of all the realism in his plays. It consists of one scene in the *Mariage d'Olympe*, the character of Seraphine in the *Lionnes Pauvres*, and the character of Maître Guérin in the piece which bears his name, for all the surrounding personages belong clearly to the world of chimæra and convention. Realism plays a much larger part in Dumas' work. *Monsieur Alphonse* is almost pure Naturalism, and the "almost" would be "quite" but for the dénouement, which reverts enthusiastically to an optimistic idealism. Dumas adored reality, and would have been an admirable observer and delineator of life if he had only had less genius. But who can prevent a man from creating when he was born to create? Who can limit the invention of a Balzac, a Dickens, a Stevenson, a Dumas *fils ?*

When Naturalism threatened to invade his own particular domain of the theatre he advanced boldly against the enemy, and devoted several prefaces to his discomfiture. Reality, as he said, is really only the dramatist's rough material, his point of departure, not his goal. Dramatic art consists in treatment and interpretation. Now Naturalism neither interprets its material nor subjects it to any process of treatment, and if it transfers a drama from the pages of a novel to the stage, it omits all those explanations which are so necessary to the spectator. A character in a Naturalist play has no right to analyse his motives in presence of the audience; indeed, how could he, when he does not know them himself? He is cut all in one piece; what he is in the first scene he remains up to the end. Then what becomes of development, and how can there be anything unforeseen, or any interest? The play either ends badly, or pretends to simulate life by having no end at all. But although a Frenchman may indulge in pessimism beside his own hearth, it appears to be an established fact that when two thousand Frenchmen are brought together in a theatre they at once become optimists; they refuse to go to bed until they have seen the deliverance of love and virtue, or at least until they have strewn a few flowers upon their bier. This, I think, is what English people call " poetic justice "; it costs nothing, and it gives a world of pleasure. In one word, a Naturalist play is not " constructed," and comes to no conclusion; hence it is neither a work of art nor a lesson in morality, whereas a good play ought to be both. If Naturalism succeeds in capturing the theatre, the theatre will cease to exist.

That was the line of argument in the camp of Dumas and Sardou. It must be admitted that the woeful and often signal failure of the most well-known novels of the Naturalist School, when transferred to the stage, seemed to justify the sort of reasoning that I have just summarised. But who could say whether the real reason of these misadventures might not be found in the simple fact that the great novelists had no sort of understanding of the theatre? We must see how

Naturalism was handled by a dramatic writer, an experiment first undertaken by M. Henry Becque.

A very curious case this of M. Henry Becque, especially to any one who has been asleep, like myself, for twenty years. When I closed my eyes there was something almost grotesque about M. Becque's position. He was knocking at the doors of all the theatres with manuscript plays that were hastily returned to him, and when he did succeed in getting a play put on the stage, people laughed till their sides ached. The experience marked an epoch and became proverbial; all the world was saying, "rire comme à *Michel Pauper.*" When I reopened my eyes to the gaslight and my ears to the gossip of the theatrical world I was rather astonished to learn that M. Henry Becque was a master, the head of a school, much debated, but largely followed and imitated; that M. Lemaître was comparing him with Molière, and that he had come forward as a candidate for the French Academy without provoking either scandal or mirth. Can M. Henry Becque's present admirers be right? Well, really, I think that they may. Then were we all wrong when

we refused to take him seriously? By no means.
I have just re-read *Michel Pauper*. It remains
what it always was—a drama full of violent ex-
aggerations, a mad sort of play, heavy withal and
so vulgar in style! The language put into the
mouths of the characters positively strikes one
dumb; the play is an altogether unique specimen
of that exasperating banality which is so often
imputed to poor M. Ohnet. A young girl, who
has been assaulted, informs us of the accident in
an antithesis which would have made my professor of rhetoric shed tears of joy: "He asked
of his own will what he could not obtain from
mine." At what possible epoch and in what sort
of society did people ever talk like that? I can
only picture to myself a group of old fogies whose
one means of communication with the spirit of
their age is the perusal of the *Petit Journal*, and
who meet thrice a week on a fourth floor looking
out into a courtyard in a blind alley somewhere
about Batignolles or the Marais to play bezique
or picquet. Let a tragedy supervene, and they
will have no way of expressing their emotions
except by recalling a few fragments of phrases

heard and only half understood in their youth. They will give you Bouchardy, combined with the insipidity of their ordinary speech, and the result will be pretty nearly the dialogue of *Michel Pauper*. But no; Bouchardy is decidedly too modern, · Bouchardy represents Romanticism brought down to the level of the illiterate spectator of 1840. M. Becque's style is much older than that. Here and there I have discovered phrases embedded in it which struck terror to my soul—fossilised epigrams of immemorial age, *mots* which date from before Madame Cottin.

To be perfectly ignorant of your own times, of the manners that prevail, the language that is spoken, the art that is cultivated and admired, of all that gives tone and commands success in society and literature, is sometimes a very great source of strength. M. Becque had that strength. Many men who isolate themselves in this fashion from the intellectual movement of their day die before their time, devoured by anger and poisoned by bitterness. Not so M. Becque. As the common folk say in Paris, "Il ne s'est pas fait de bile"; he was never at a loss for amusement, for he made quite as merry over the world as the world could over him. Like Horace's peasant, he waited for the river to cease flowing, and lo and behold, the river dried up !

He might have sought to learn from Scribe the secret of the "well-constructed" play; he, the hundredth in succession to Dumas *fils*, might have tried his hand at a "problem play," with a happy ending; he preferred to spend the leisure of a rejected author in re-reading Molière and in observing life. Molière and Life; surely two pretty good masters ? They appear to have taught M. Becque that nothing interests us or amuses us so much as to see people unconsciously engaged in a blind pursuit of their own advantage or passion whithersoever it leads them, or to hear them reveal themselves "without wishing it or knowing it," in phrases whose true bearing they fail to catch. Note that even the hypocrites use such phrases; otherwise we should not know that Tartufe was Tartufe until he unmasked. Now take one of these characters and place him in a situation which brings his besetting sin, his master passion into play. Then leave him to himself; don't, on any account, interfere, or you will spoil everything. No complication, no catastrophe, nothing but the development of character. Above all, no intervention on the part of Providence. In the fourth act of *L'Etrangère* Rémonin tells us that he is expecting something. "The gods will come," he says, and assuredly in the fifth act something does happen and the gods appear. Well, in M. Becque's plays the gods never appear; men get along as they can. How does one know when the play is over? Why, the curtain falls. And when does the curtain fall? When the author has drawn out of his characters all that they are capable of in a given situation. This, in its main outlines, is the dramatic system whose masterpieces so far have been *Les Corbeaux* and *La Parisienne*.

Death has made a sudden incursion into a Parisian family, and carried off the head of the house in the full tide of his activity, before he had time to set his affairs in order. The widow and the three daughters of the dead man are thereby left exposed to all the criminal devices which are made possible by the settlement of a much encumbered property. The crows swoop down upon them—their father's partner, the lawyer, the architect, the tradespeople. The four women would be simply devoured if the eldest girl did not happen to find favour in the eyes of one of the birds of prey, old Teissier. She marries this detestable individual to save her mother and sisters; she marries him without any tears or fuss, *sans faire d'histoires*, for she is a practical girl, and this sort of sacrifice is common enough in France. Do the audience insist upon a conclusion? Well, if the crows are upon you, you must seek the protection of the biggest and blackest, so that he may make short work of the others. Teissier says naïvely to Marie, "Ah, my poor child, since your father's death you have been surrounded by rascals!" But let it not be forgotten that of all the rascals, he has been the most greedy and the most dangerous.

That is M. Becque's idea of comedy, and those are the sort of phrases he indulges in; monstrous utterances which seem perfectly simple to those who utter them. These *mots* abound in *La Parisienne.* Clotilde has a husband and a lover; she proposes to make them both happy, to be both a good wife and a good mistress, and to carry on her quiet little *ménage à trois* with the most careful regard for appearances. She appropriates three days a week to temperament: the rest belongs to family life, to society, to "duty," to virtue. It is a cold-blooded, comfortable, commuted sort of adultery, which thinks itself respectable, because it has gone on a long time—an adultery which reasons and calculates and moralises and goes to mass. "You would not wish," says Clotilde to Lafont, "to have a mistress with no religion. It would be horrible!" She reproaches him for his lukewarmness in the relationship which her fancy has invented for him. "You do not love my husband, you do not love my husband." And he defends himself hotly against this original accusation. If she has some fancy over and above the recognised lover, she justifies it in her own eyes by making it serve the advancement of her husband. Listen to the virtuous indignation of the lover, who, under these circumstances, is a hundredfold more marital than the husband himself: " Resist it, Clotilde ; that is the only honourable course, and the only course worthy of you ! " These phrases made the first audiences who heard them gnash their teeth ; now they are often compared with Molière's epigrams. You can smile if you like, but you may also weep. *La Parisienne* is an example of that disagreeable kind of vaudeville which could be converted into a serious drama by a mere nothing—a note left on a table, or the sudden opening of a door. *Les Corbeaux*, unlike the plays of Dumas and his school, is a serious drama, which comes very near to ending in comedy.

This would be the moment for holding M. Becque up to public reprobation in the sacred name of morality, but it is useless to count on me for that purpose. My own view is simply this. Marriage, as we see it nowadays, defaced and corrupted by modern life, seems to me almost as contemptible as adultery. Restore its sincerity, its pristine beauty and sublimity, and I shall be in the front rank of its defenders. Our morality has been so perverted and dragged in the mire by our system of compromise, that it cannot, perhaps, serve any higher purpose than the ignoble ends of a Clotilde and a Lafont. I for one shall not expend the thousandth part of a drop of ink in defending either the institution, or the social order which is reared on such a basis.

There remains the question of artistic merit. To my mind M. Becque's rupture with convention and theatrical devices is by no means so complete as he says and as he wishes us to believe. Take *Les Corbeaux* for example. I could twit M. Becque with a certain episode which introduces a suggestion of somewhat conventional melodrama into a corner of his very realistic -play, a reminiscence of the ill-fated *Michel Pauper*. But I prefer to attack the play directly and in virtue of M. Becque's own principles, for up to a certain point I am ready to recognise those principles as sound, valid, and far-reaching. Four women are imprisoned in a circle, whence there is no possible escape, alone with the birds of prey. They have nothing in the shape of a man to defend them. Why? Because M. Becque has elected to send the son to his regiment, and because he has also been pleased to make the *fiancé* of one of the girls a wretched coward. In default of such natural defenders, salvation might have been sought in some other incident; Marie, for instance, might have proved attractive to a different sort of man, or the much-talked-of estate might have tempted another speculator to make a higher bid, and the crows would have been forced to fly away without their dinner. The gods don't always come, but, after all, they do come sometimes. In any case life is for ever creating diversions, which thwart all kinds of projects, the schemes of rogues as well as those of honest men. M. Becque arrests the march of events so as to leave the field clear for the unfolding of his characters. He is within his rights as a dramatic author. I only want to prove that even he subjects that raw slice cut out of life to some sort of culinary process, before calling upon us to swallow and digest it.

Still, there is quite enough that is fresh and

daring in Henry Becque's system and in his dramatic work to justify the assertion that he has created something. He has really begotten a child, and, as Musset says :—

"C'est déjà bien joli quand on en a fait un."

Only I could have wished the baby to receive a prettier name from its godfathers and god-mothers. Too late, for *La Parisienne* and all the plays of that school have been christened *comédie rosse.*

This word "rosse" is of Spanish origin : and, like almost every word that changes its nation-ality, it acquired a depreciatory and offensive sense when it crossed the Pyrenees, testifying thereby to the stupid contempt which different nations feel for one another. Perhaps, too, the name of Don Quixote's horse contributed some-what to the suggestion of insult attaching to the French expression. However that may be, a "rosse" is a jade or a screw, and in this sense, during the seventeenth century, the word crept into literary use, for I remember both a line of Scarron and one of Boileau in which

it occurs.   In the present century the word
was first applied to a certain sort of woman—
an insult so vile that it must first have occurred
to some stable boy who had had a quarrel
with his mistress.   From the wine shop it
passed to the smoking-room, since there are
moments when even a man, who prides
himself on his good breeding, will behave
like a drunken coachman.   In such moods he is
glad enough to cast words savouring of the
gutter or the shambles in the face of the woman
whom he no longer loves, to revenge himself for
ever having loved her.   Once she had every
charm, now she has every vice.   She is a liar
and a deceiver, she has no heart, she is "une
rosse" or simply "rosse," for the word may be
both substantive and adjective.   It only remained
for the poor degraded word to be applied to a
literary style, and this application has now been
made.   The *comédie rosse* is not only a comedy
which gives the heroine a villainous part; *rosserie*
extends to all the characters, and, in fact, consists
in simple lack of conscience.   *Rosserie* is a
vicious sort of ingenuousness; it represents the

state of mind of people who have never had any moral sense, and who are as much at home amid impurity and injustice as a fish is in the sea. It is a sort of childlike and heavenly repose in an atmosphere of corruption, which suggests a travesty of the Golden Age—a world in which all our principles of morality are reversed, and where, in the words of Milton's Satan, evil has become good. This reign of evil is inaugurated without any noisy revolution, without any apparent change in family or social relations, or in ordinary conversation; it is brought about by a gradual diversion of modern ideas from their original source, until they end by justifying all the crimes against which they were at first directed. Imagine a society which retains the Decalogue as its moral code and guides its actions by the Seven Deadly Sins.

I said just now that we had a kind of literature to which the name *rosse* may be applied. I ought to have said that we had two. Indeed, I think that the *chanson rosse* preceded the *comédie rosse.* Mdlle. Yvette Guilbert has done much to shed lustre upon this kind of song, which, thanks to her, has become an article of export. That curious talent of hers was displayed upon a London stage, together with her characteristic costumes and attitudes, and the Gigolos and Gigolettes have no further secrets for those who saw Yvette at the Empire. I do not wish to force the point, but, as Renan is said to have admired her and paid her compliments, I am justified in mentioning her as a symptom.

The *chanson rosse* first saw the light at the *Chat Noir*, that far-famed *Chat Noir* which has been almost eclipsed by its innumerable imitators but which maintained its pre-eminence for ten years. At first it was merely a wine shop in Montmartre, the resort of the poets and painters of the quarter. They formed a more amiable and better bred Bohemia than the Bohemia of old, less addicted to smashing window panes or tying cats by their tails to bell ropes, and less enamoured of brutal nocturnal frolics, but more revolutionary in their views on art and literature than the Bohemia of Mürger and Champfleury. "Passant, sois moderne," was the significant legend inscribed over the door, and before they had well crossed the threshold, the proprietor of the place, Rodolphe Salis, a man of fine phrases and large gestures, pelted distinguished visitors with such stupefying sentences as " Montmartre, the brains of Paris, is proud to clasp its sons to her bosom." The visitors sat down ; and waiters, dressed like members of the Institute, rushed to serve the new comers. This prostitution of the venerable green - sprigged frock - coat of the Academy shows pretty clearly the contempt felt for classic art, *l'art poncif* or *pompier*, as it was called. The *Chat Noir* had unwittingly become a theatre—the dwellers in it contributed their personality and their wit. Men of the world crowded to these strange spectacles; all Paris was there listening to Meusy, Emile Goudeau, Mac Nab, and Jean Ramsan singing their own songs, babyish refrains, military ballads, neo-Hellenic odes, idylls of the barriers, which, for all their apparent triviality, contained incredible refinements of literary virtuosity. Then came the Chinese shadow dances of Caran d'Ache, who could defile before you the whole drama of the great Napoleon, with nothing but a luminous circle a few inches in diameter and some silhouettes cut out in tin and moving behind a piece of calico.

Another day you had the temptation of St. Anthony according to Flaubert—a stupendous philosophical comedy embracing the whole of modern life, and Jules Lemaître, sitting before these suggestive shadows, thought of the shadows passing to and fro in Plato's cave. On another evening, Willette—the Watteau of Montmartre, but a Watteau who never finished his drawings because he preferred to retain the *flou*, the vaguely fluctuating outlines of a dream—brought his friends to the *Chat Noir* to see a rope-dancing pantomime which displayed his beloved Pierrot under the strangest aspect, together with a columbine of an entirely new type, destined to replace Grévin's Parisienne *grisette*, just as she in her turn had displaced Marcellin's type, the successor of the Parisienne according to Tony Johannot. A face with a fugitive pallor, and a modest, caressing grace, half mocking, half sad, hair falling over her eyes, and arms of exquisite slenderness, feet encased in black silk stockings and dear little shoes, shooting up like rockets in a whirlwind of muslin and lace, the famous "*dessous*," which fill so large a place in the dreams of bachelors and the budget of married men. Tinchant, the poetical pianist, was the orchestra, Rodolphe Salis explained the *tableaux* in a Charentonesque style; pictures, words and music helped out each other's meaning and blended in a harmonious whole. What suggestive veins of raillery, what new ideas were to be met with, and what wild theories were broached in those early gatherings at the *Chat Noir!* Now, if ever, was the moment to set about some serious undertaking, and in due time appeared the Théâtre Libre to make the attempt.

III.

THE THÉÂTRE LIBRE.

On a chilly October evening in 1887, a few cabs from the heart of Paris painfully crawled up the street to Montmartre, and a handful of men, carefully buttoned up in thick overcoats, peered about them and plunged with no little hesitation into a narrow, very muddy, and dimly lighted alley. Hovels to right and left, in front an indistinct vision of a staircase. This was the place. The cabs brought the fashionable world which hungers after literary novelties; the buttoned-up men were critics who came to worship—or to spurn— the nascent art in its cradle. In default of a star, these great-coated Magi were reduced to asking their way at the wine-shop in the Place Pigalle; at least that was the fate which befell M. Jules Lemaître, who has given the emotions awakened by the journey a permanent place in literary history. Do you want more precise details? The doubtful-looking alley had a name no less high-sounding than the Passage de l'Elysée des Beaux-Arts, and the Théâtre Libre, on that particular evening, had its local habitation at No. 37.

A word or two as to its material resources. The spectators were all subscribers with season tickets, and were, therefore, almost as much at home as the members of a club. The mere fact of taking no money at the doors freed the theatre from all the regulations which govern public entertainments. In the eye of the law, the Théâtre Libre was not a theatre at all; consequently its promoters were quite at liberty to bid defiance to the Censorship. Besides, as no piece could be played more than three times, it was not necessary to secure the continued attendance of the average playgoer. Provided that something new or startling, and hitherto unknown, was presented to the few hundred rich cockneys, whose curiosity served to support the venture, all would go well; and, under these conditions, daring was not only desirable but absolutely necessary. There was one drawback which had not been foreseen, but which, in the long run, made itself felt. The house was so entirely composed of friends or avowed enemies, of the initiated or scoffers, that it seldom gave a frank or spontaneous verdict. There is not, and there never can be, any real success except that which is attested by the vulgar pence of the vulgar public; but it took a little time for the world to find that out.

The name of the manager of the Théâtre Libre, a comparatively unknown actor called Antoine, was soon to be in the mouths of all Paris. He was more than brusque in speech and manner, violently dictatorial in fact, and the strangest of bedfellows, as those whom necessity forced to associate with him were quick to perceive; but he possessed that degree of self-confidence and contempt for his predecessors which appears to be the first requisite for an innovator. What did he mean to do? First of all to upset all traditions of acting and *mise-en-scène*. In his eyes the stage ought to be, as Ibsen said, merely a room with one partition knocked down so that the spectators can see what is going on in it. Thence it follows that all the action cannot be carried on with the actor's face to the audience. Antoine, indeed, very often turned his back, and people laughed long and loudly. To a great many of the clever folk of Paris, Antoine's back-turning represented the Théâtre Libre. For all that, this back had its own way of acting, and was very significant in certain situations. The lesson was by no means lost upon the artist world, quick to understand and to imitate; and in this, as in many other respects, Antoine's unavowed or unconscious disciples included actors much superior to himself, who took good care to profit by his example, and at the same time to tone down what was aggravating and aggressive in his methods.

Antoine had no special gift for the studied delivery of effective phrases, after the fashion of the Samsons and Regniers, but he set to work to discover the dominant characteristic which constituted the essential unity of any human being: some one of the deadly sins, perhaps—at least one which lends itself to dramatic purposes, such as avarice, pride, luxury, egotism; and, above all,

the love of life and the fear of death. When he
had once grasped this leading feature, every
word, every movement, every glance, was made
to translate it into a form that could be felt.   A
method so sustained and intense created an impression strong enough to supply the place of
all the manifold explanations of Dumas' and
Augier's plays. Seeing is sometimes more than
understanding, and those who saw Antoine as
Morel in Léon Hennique's *Esther Brandès* can
never recall it without a shudder. From the
very first scene we knew the man could not live,
that his malady was a sort of petrifaction of the
heart, and that the fatal termination, which was
inevitable, might be brought on prematurely by
any violent emotion. It was impossible, looking
at Antoine, to forget for a single moment that
heart turning into stone, or to escape from
the agonising fear lest the deadly emotion,
which constantly threatened, should descend like
the blade of the guillotine. One saw the doomed
man struggling against physical pain, or yielding
to it in pure abjectness, alternating between
confidence and bitterness, passion and lamenta-

tion, weak tenderness and fierce egotism. One felt his deliberate efforts at calmness, his false resignation, his sincere illusions, the way in which his whole moral nature had shrunk, and been warped and deformed, by the fear of on-coming death. It was at the close of an evening like this that M. Emile Faguet, at that time dramatic critic to the *Soleil*, discovered in M. Antoine "some of the elements of a great actor."

Round him gathered a troop of mere school-boys and schoolgirls made living by his strong personality. The feeling of having a cause to advance, and a systematic campaign to carry on —a series of battles, that is to say, to be fought on ground chosen beforehand, and under the eyes of a select audience—gave their acting, as the same critic assures us, a certain "fire and con-centration" that would never have been found elsewhere.

What was to be attempted with these tools? Antoine's programme was perfectly definite. He knew very well what he wanted, and still better what he did not want. Nothing could be more explicit or more valuable, as a means of disclosing both his sympathies and his antipathies, than a letter written by him in 1894 to M. Camille Fabre. He gave an enthusiastic welcome to a MS. play submitted to him by this young author, whom he called "one of the most gifted and best-balanced minds of the age." It was a long time, he told him, since he had had "such a mouthful to nibble at"; nevertheless he made reservations, foresaw "the objections which the advanced critics would not fail to raise." His sketch of M. Fabre's manner paints him to the life. "Your method is Becque's, and you enshrine your very curious conception in the antiquated forms of Dumas and Sardou. There is the fag-end of a problem in your first act, and your two parallel threads you borrow, very likely without knowing it, from the author of *La Haine*" (Sardou). But Antoine gave unqualified praise to "the firm outlines of the figures and characters." It is amusing to notice that this "mouthful" which Antoine was so happy to "nibble at" he never attempted to play. But the piece survives, and so does the letter—it is the syllabus of the Théâtre Libre. Above all, no compromise with the school of the "well constructed " play, the play with explanations and a gradual working up. No subplot, no problem, no contrasts, no moral : nothing but implacable reality and unflinching unity. The drama is a mere procession of human types, a gallery of walking portraits. As for situations, why trouble about them ? They arise quite naturally out of the most ordinary circumstances of life : the relations subsisting between members of the same family; a marriage, coming into an inheritance, a bankruptcy, or the vulgarest form of adultery —any one of these is quite enough. Life offers us such adventures at every step, but the stage, up to now, has presented them in the falsest light possible, because dramatic authors might as well have waited for the Greek Kalends as tried to perform the impossible feat of " creating " situations.

I have largely reconstituted the *répertoire* of the Théâtre Libre by collecting some sixty plays, a good half of which belong to the school of Henry Becque, that is to say, the School of

Naturalism modified to suit the requirements of the stage. Amongst the most distinguished of this group of authors, the first places must be assigned to Jean Jullien, Pierre Wolff, Léon Hennique, George Ancey, Brieux, and Camille Fabre, for M. Antoine consoled the last-named for his first discomfiture by playing a very striking play of his, *L'Argent.* Not that these authors formed a *coterie* quite as distinct as the Romantic school of the Place Royale in 1830; indeed, they very possibly did not know one another; but they breathed the same air, fed on the same ideas, and drank of the same springs on their journey towards the same point on the literary horizon. There is such a family likeness between their plays, and such a community of system and intention, that they seem like a continuation of each other. A feature, which has been indicated or outlined in an earlier play, is corrected and completed in a second, and I do not think that it would be very difficult to analyse the class as a whole, just as one might analyse a single play by picking out here and there some detail, or character, or phrase, or fragment of a scene from the most striking works of the school and the period. By those I understand the plays which do sincerely aim at what is new or what is best; I leave out of account the formless productions which are nothing but an insult to men of sense. The first thing that surprises us is the absence of all *exposition.* No *exposition!* What an omission, what a blow to the dramatic authors brought up in the school of Scribe! The *exposition* had served not only to reveal the initial situation—one scene would have done for that—but to present the characters in such a fashion that there would be no need to come back to them; the rest of the play followed as necessarily as the conclusion of a syllogism from the juxtaposition of the major and minor premiss. The author expended upon it all the talent and brilliancy that he could muster; the first act was generally given up to it, and sometimes the second and third. Indeed, it contained the play in embryo; it announced it and related its substance like the ancient Prologue. It was often as much superior to the play itself as the mountebank's speech at the door is to the spectacle provided inside the booth at a fair.

There was nothing of this sort at the Théâtre Libre. Far from enlightening us, the first act generally led us completely astray. Take, for example, *La Sérénade*, by Jean Jullien. When the wife of a watchmaker, seated behind her counter, tells us that she " thirsts for the ideal " and longs for " the love of a poet," and when we see that this poet is a pretentious usher, who teaches her little boy the Latin declensions, we imagine ourselves in for a vaudeville, and are convinced that the shade of Labiche hovers over us. In the second act we plunge into pure drama, and what a drama! It touches the borders even of incest, and we ask ourselves how the author is going to get out of the difficulty without wholesale butchery. But just as we are beginning to take these jewellers in earnest, as if they were Atrides or Labdacides, lo and behold, they think better of it and get reconciled. The guilty mother marries her daughter to her lover, and they all drink champagne to the health of the future couple. In fact, we have slipped back into farce in the most lamentable fashion possible. There is the same shock in M. George Ancey's play, *La Dupe*, only he manages it more skilfully, and his intention to make merry at our expense is less openly visible. We first assist at what in matrimonial slang is called an "interview," one of those meetings which experts in such matters know how to bring about between a girl in search of a husband and a young man in search of a dowry. Albert Bonnel makes the usual fatuous remarks, and we quite understand that the poor girl takes a dislike to him. We are spared none of the silly phrases that are likely to occur in such a conversation. "The cold is really abnormal. I don't know if it means to last." According to the old logic of the stage, the man who asked such a question was invariably a good fellow, and no one had any doubt as to the fate which awaited him when he married. But M. George Ancey reverses the probabilities. In the second act we find Adèle married to Albert, and it is she who is madly in love with him, and he who deceives her. This utterer of solemn platitudes turns out to be a monster, a humorous monster withal, full of gaiety and lively chatter. He jokes with his mother-in-law, and makes her laugh till she cries, before robbing her of her money. And we took him for a harmless simpleton!

I am amazed, but not altogether displeased, for, after all, astonishment is half the pleasure one expects to get out of the theatre, and, like all my contemporaries, I am tired of those over-logical plays, in which everything is clear from the very first scene, and the action runs as smoothly as a tramcar on rails. The French are well known to have sometimes insisted upon the distinction between tragedy and comedy with a rigour which the Greeks would not have understood, and which has never been known in England. In our age the distinction has disappeared, and I have pointed out that in Dumas' and Augier's composite plays drama often succeeds comedy in one and the same play. But such poetical license in theatrical matters must follow the German gastronomic maxim which allows wine after beer but forbids beer after wine. The two elements must alternate in an invariable order. The peculiarity of the Théâtre Libre, as we have just seen, consists in the reversal of this order; but it also consists in the mixture of comedy and tragedy in one and the same character. You have laughable rogues and tragic idiots; you have, in short, the idea of transient absurdity substituted for that of permanent absurdity. The same individual makes us laugh, and then tremble, and then laugh again. He passes from one phase to another, though preserving his identity, and rings the changes between the awe-inspiring and the grotesque. Nothing like this had ever been seen on any stage, except Punch's stage or Shakespeare's, the only two really complete and comprehensive forms of drama which we possess. None but children and philosophers can both laugh and cry over the same things and the same people.

M. George Ancey's *La Dupe* might be read by those who are not too much hampered by English ways of thinking, as a specimen of naturalist art and the Gospel according to Henry Becque. No one can fail to recognise a certain power in this fantastic and complicated sketch of a personage, who poses before his victims, who claims their admiration, and who is a complete master of comfortable vice and of the art of sparing himself the trouble, never the shame, of lying. He complains to his wife of his mistress's extravagance, just as he complains to his mistress of his wife's exactingness. He is amiable and placid, has a joke or a song on his lips, as long as he gets money; but he becomes a perfect monster when it is refused. What a flood of rage and hate pours forth, what a stream of low, venomous, and cruel insults, when this beast in human form is let loose! I believe the type a real one, I must sorrowfully admit that I even believe it common. How many homes, which appear almost happy, conceal like depths of grief and degradation!

By no means all the writers for the Théâtre Libre can draw character with such clear and firm lines as M. George Ancey. Many either have not the gift, or allow it to lie unused. Look at M. Léon Hennique's *Esther Brandès*, which belongs to the class of enigmatical plays. I have already mentioned it as one in which intrigues both of love and of self-interest are carried on round a dying man. In the middle of it all is stationed a frigid and mysterious old maid, with a piece of knitting or embroidery in her hand on all occasions. She sees everything, superintends everything, brings affairs to their proper termination, and never gives her own ideas on the subject. What does she want? To save her young sister, or to ruin her? To protect her against her own impulses, or to rob her of her lover? At the last I grasp the fact that she has killed her brother-in-law in consequence of a sudden impulse, so that he may not bequeath a hundred thousand francs to a stranger; but I am not at all clear as to the person she is working for, and I could not say whether she has really been the good or the evil genius of the family. If I complained of this uncertainty to the author, he would probably reply that it is so because it is so, and that I had no right to any explanation. Life is as it may be; it has no need to justify itself for being what it is.

M. Jullien goes further in *La Sérénade*. The

wretch who seduces Madame Cottin and her daughter is a perfect nonentity, a model of banality, I had almost said of vulgar conventionality. There is nothing remarkable about him except a rather flowery style of talking, a discreet combination of the novel of fine sentiments and a specimen piece of college rhetoric. The hero of *La Dupe* was at least a somebody ; this man is a mere nobody. We were used to the idea that a great criminal could be "a character," and it is rather hard to get rid of the notion. Still, it has got to be done, and though the symptom is a serious one, there is nothing surprising about it, for whereas Dumas' and Augier's dramatic work corresponded, as I pointed out, to Cousin's philosophy, Becque and his disciples try to bring their work into line with the philosophy of Taine. The result is the complete disappearance of human personality : it is the death of the ego, its reabsorption into the non-ego.

Be it understood that I am here speaking of the ego viewed as an independent cause and a free agent, of the ego that wills, not the ego that feels. That ego is located in the skin, and the purely animal form of egoism, which is its resultant expression, asserts itself boldly enough in the plays of the Théâtre Libre. You can hear it bursting out just as you hear your dog squeal when you tread on its toes, or your cat when she is on her way to a rendezvous on the roofs. Moreover, the Théâtre Libre represents almost exclusively the class which is generally considered the most egotistic, the *petite bourgeoisie.* What is really remarkable is that there is nothing to indicate whether we are in Paris or the provinces. The way in which the literary world of thirty years ago idolised the civilisation of the boulevards is absolutely unknown amongst the younger men. To them Paris is nothing but a vast assemblage of houses, a place with a number of churches, banks, schools, cafés; the Boulevard sinks into a street planted with trees, much too brightly lighted, and far too crowded. As a symbol the Boulevard is played out. The *dramatis personæ* of the Théâtre Libre are either real provincials, or Parisian provincials, who wear themselves to death in a lifelong struggle to amass a few five-franc pieces. Their dream is to buy an estate, some hideous building, which travesties a Gothic castle or a Chinese pagoda, and culminates in a belvedere with coloured glass in its windows, commanding "a beautiful view." On Sunday they play at bowls in shirt sleeves, whilst the railway whistle shrieks in the middle of the air from *Lakmé* which their daughter is strumming.

Ménages d'artistes, written by M. Brieux, shows me clearly that the literary Bohemian, for all his aspirations towards a higher life and an ideal of independence, belongs, at any rate in the person of his wife, to this petty prosaic business world. This world is very close to the people; but yesterday it was one with them, at any rate its relations were, if not itself. It preserves their sentiments and way of talking, even when its fortune is made. M. Albert Bonnel is the manager of an insurance company with a salary of 30,000 francs a year; but when he insults and beats his wife, after having ruined and betrayed her, wherein does he differ from the working man, who does the same when he comes home drunk on Monday evening? Some sort of equilibrium between the two extremes of the class is indeed maintained by the fact that some are sinking down by reason of their own weight, the inherent heaviness of their nature, and the incurable coarseness of their desires, whilst others are ceaselessly impelled by an unquenchable ambition to rise. This ambition, which is characteristic of our democratic age, has never been better painted than in *Blanchette*, another piece by M. Brieux, which has in it the elements of a masterpiece.

Blanchette is the daughter of a village tavern-keeper. She has been educated in a boarding school for "young ladies," the daughters of the *bourgeoisie*. She has passed her examination as a teacher and won her diploma. Père Rousset has this bit of official paper framed and hung up in the most conspicuous place in his tavern. He obliges every person who enters to admire the magic parchment, and his respect for his daughter verges on adoration. She knows everything, understands everything; she can give lessons to all the world; the schoolmaster himself would not dare to dispute with her. But when Père Rousset perceives that the situation, to which in his eyes the famous diploma gives her a right, halts by the way, even if it is ever coming at all, he turns round abruptly and completely, with all the blind fury of the savage who insults and breaks his fetish, if it has not sent rain and fine weather as he wanted them. He is as hard and brutal to his daughter as he had been admiring and respectful. "Ah! miserable good - for - nothing, you shall serve the customers, and let us have no idling about it!" And when she resists, he turns her out of the house. She is abandoned to chance, a prey to every temptation and every form of suffering. One more *déclassée* in the Paris streets, who will be forced to sell her love for bread, since she cannot live on her diploma. Yet these people are not all wicked. Here comes in one of the ideas which inspire this school of play-writers: fate and society are the sole causes of the sins of individuals.

The same conception recurs in all the serious work of that group at that period. We feel that the world has woke up in a fright during the

night and discovered that the pillars upon which
it rests are rotten and ready to be swept away by
a subterranean inundation. All our principles
are falsified, our institutions perverted, our ideas
somehow distorted. Morality, whether public or
private, has been entirely reversed, and now seeks
to justify and conceal the wrongs and the degra-
dations that it ought to expose. There is a perpetual discord between principles and practice.
Our father tells us to respect the goods of others
whilst he is ceaselessly engaged in robbery. Our
mother orders us to tell the truth, and lies from
morning till night. This deceit and chicanery
gradually poisons our whole being; we are for
ever talking of reason, virtue, pity, but our
hearts are full of nothing but base and sordid
self-interest. Do you know why Madame Viot
in the first act of *La Dupe* decides to marry
her daughter to Albert Bonnel, and why she is
in such a hurry to see the marriage accomplished?
Don't be taken in, whatever you do, by the
weighty and sentimental, or specious and touching
considerations that she puts forward. This is the
true reason : she has taken a suite of rooms for

herself, and she wishes to hand over the end of her lease to her future son-in-law. If she is to lose nothing the marriage must take place before the April quarter. To deny the possibility, nay, the probability, of such a scheme is to know very little of the French *petite bourgeoisie ;* it is a small matter and rather comic, but the misery of a lifetime is the outcome of it.

"La famille, c'est l'argent," says one of the characters in the play with this title which M. Fabre had played at the Théâtre Libre. It depicted the members of a family manœuvring round its chief as he made his will. Interest divided them, then brought them together, and dispersed them again, and again united them. They do not admit their evil designs even to themselves, for the very good reason that they are unconscious of them. Nor do they say with Racine's Narcisse:

"Pour nous rendre heureux, perdons les misérables !"

No one ever did say that, not even Narcisse, and it was very *naïf* of us to go on so long admiring such psychology. The members of the Reynard family are neither cynics, properly so-called, nor genuine hypocrites. Madame Reynard has had a lover for fifteen years, and her conscience has got hardened because the affair is of such long standing. Her daughter Mathilde, who is on the point of taking a lover herself, is not a whit more disposed to be lenient to her mother's fault on that account. Roux, who stirs up Mathilde to denounce her mother, thinks himself the most honest fellow in the world. When he has secured the infamy in question he embraces Mathilde tenderly: "Dear little woman, how charming you are!" Then, having completely demolished his mother-in-law, he perceives that it is to his interest to set her on her legs again. Which he does, but taking good care to make the gift revocable, and reserving to himself the power of withdrawing every concession which he has made. There is no display of ill-feeling, only the precautions which a careful man takes for the future, nothing more. His views on social respectability, the happiness of living in unity, and the duties of religion are honest and plausible. You would say as much yourself in a similar case. The family almost goes down on its knees to entreat the adulterous woman to remain by the hearth which she has outraged, but which she alone is now in a position to save from ruin. She makes conditions, and they are accepted, but with a secret resolution to break through them. All these people, who have insulted, robbed, and betrayed each other, and whose hearts are filled with evil thoughts, propose to resume their life together, until a wretched sum of 2,000 francs fans the dying quarrel into a flame. Just at that moment luncheon is announced. "Let us go in," says the father ; "we can talk of this again after lunch." And that is the end. One knows that they will go on chained together, perpetually distrusting one another and disputing with one another. What they were yesterday they will be to-morrow.

These few examples serve to show the principal tenets of this school. The authors were young, some of them had talent, very many were quite sincere in their hatred for the art of the preceding generation, and on a great many points they had right on their side as against the principles of Dumas and Augier. Their philosophy was sound and well thought out, their view of life and society cruel but just. Nevertheless the school has failed, and after a few short hours of stormy notoriety it fell into discredit, almost into oblivion, even before the Théâtre Libre had closed its doors. Its chief standard bearers have vanished or become converted to another style. Death has thinned the ranks fast during the last few years, and the grass is already green on the grave of dramatic naturalism.

This defeat is due, in the first place, to what M. Brunetière called the bankruptcy of naturalism in fiction. Bankruptcy might be thought rather a hard word, were it not for the memory of the proud hopes and magnificent promises of its outset. It has only taken ten years to exhaust its apparently boundless popularity, and ten more years to scatter the Médan school in every sense of the word. Guy de Maupassant is no more, Huysmans has retired into learned seclusion and the microscopic investigation of certain special *milieux*, Edouard Rod has diverged very far from his original starting point, and the public's stubborn refusal to read the works of Paul Alexis does it infinite honour. Even M. Zola has greatly changed. More than half the pages of *La Débâcle* and *Rome* have nothing in common with naturalism, nay, are almost its negation.

Besides, even if that peculiar form of naturalism, which M. Becque's pupils had imposed upon the Théâtre Libre, was no longer borne on by the mighty intellectual tide from without, it had its own inherent source of weakness, its germs of dissolution. After all, it may be impossible to construct plays without situations, or characters, or a conclusion. Still, nothing did so much harm to the naturalist plays as the ineptitude of their partisans. Every criticism of that day shows us how insensible the public was to the hidden meaning of the plays, or to such traits of nature as they contained; it was merely on the look-out for risky phrases, which it greeted with acclamation. No art could resist such stupid admiration; it is a disgrace even to have deserved it. If the author—like M. de Gramont in *Rolande*—set up the image of Good opposite that of Evil, the company received it coldly, and became delirious in their delight over objectionable scenes. Their laughter deprived the satire of all bitterness, and converted what had come near to being a sermon into an impure form of amusement.

But the rising generation, which had been given *Germinal* and *La Terre* for its moral and literary pabulum, was already giving place to a still younger generation, which devoured Bourget's novels and the articles of the Vicomte de Vogué. A wave of passionate curiosity, like that which about 1825 threw France into the arms of Goethe and Byron, now swept it towards Tolstoi and Dostoieffsky, Ibsen and Björnson. After the Russians the Norwegians; after the Norwegians the Germans. The women of the "monde où l'on s'ennuie" threw themselves into the movement. You heard a woman talking about "giving her soul a Norwegian colouring" when probably she had no soul at all. Others saw the drama of the future in Maeterlinck's symbolism and expected *L'Intruse* to wake in them the same kind of shudder that their grandfathers had found in the *Nouvelles Extraordinaires* of Edgar Poe. Stendhal's admirers severed themselves from the naturalist school, and the psychological novel triumphed all along the line. Mysticism came to its own again, in accordance with the reaction against the excesses of realism which it was easy enough to foresee. The world lost itself in that vague and neutral region stretching from Charcot to Madame Blavatsky; people talked hypnotism, suggestion, telepathy, till they got to talking miracles. Republican society underwent a curious evolution. Its leaders had not all had fathers; but they had almost always sons and daughters, and were beginning to have grandchildren. That is the fatal moment. When men sit looking complaisantly at their families, they bethink them that there is a great deal to be said for heredity. Their wives develop a thirst for what is respectable, even for what is *chic*, and draw insensibly closer to the aristocracy of birth, which has lost nothing by the Republic; it has gained on the contrary, for old parchment has acquired an enormous value in Vanity Fair since the manufacture of it has come to an end. A political event has favoured this fusion of classes. A very clever Pope perceived that though the union of the throne with the altar profited both while both remained erect, it was but a snare and a delusion when the altar alone remained intact and the throne lay in the dust. It is not meet to bind the living to the dead; therefore the Sovereign Pontiff hastened to cut the cords. Since then the priesthood has acted as mediator between the aristocracy and the ruling classes, and the Church has become neutral ground. Thither the world flocks, as it flocks to the Opéra Comique, for matrimonial "interviews." The daughter of M. le Ministre sits at a ball or a charity meeting side by side with a La Tremoille, and his son has his coat cut after the fashion prescribed by the Prince de Sagan. This is what is called "the new spirit," or better still, "the return to religion."

Like every other form of evolution, it has its counterpart in literature. Whilst the churches provide spectacles accompanied by opera singers and processions like those of the *Biche au Bois*, the theatres — even those of the Foire — play mysteries after the manner of Oberammergau. Neither the writers of these mysteries, nor the actors, nor the public which goes to see them are inspired either by the spirit of parody or of devotion. They are as far removed from Voltaire as from Veuillot. Religious emotion is to them only an artistic sensation like any other; they try its flavour and exploit it, and then they go back to the filthy dens of Montmartre, where the police make periodical raids calculated not to put its frequenters to too great inconvenience. Their Christianity is a Christianity *à la* Baudelaire, lulled by bells and soothed by incense, seeing in the Magdalen only another "dame aux camélias," whose golden hair, borrowed from Flemish art, awakens beautiful dreams. At bottom this section of society remains profoundly sensual. In practice it is more pagan than Rome in the year 200, and when Tolstoi sets before it the Christian ideal in its pristine severity, it recoils with horror and demands a cold douche or even a strait waistcoat for the man who has dared to frighten it.

We have seen the fixed and exclusive character of Antoine's ideas with regard to dramatic literature. Nevertheless he did not fail to throw the doors of his theatre wide open to all the opposing streams and the currents crossing in the air which might give birth to germs. Traditions and original plays, in verse and prose, symbolic, exotic, archaic developments, all found favour in his eyes. He played the forgotten pieces of yesterday alternately with the famous pieces of to-morrow, and even old plays which by virtue of their age had grown young again. He it was who allowed Paris to become acquainted with Léon Tolstoi's *Power of Darkness* and Ibsen's *Ghosts.* He gave us *Le Pain du Péché*, a somewhat strongly flavoured Provençal legend by Aubanel, translated and dramatised by Paul Arène; *La Reine Fiammette*, too, by Catulle Mendès, a fantastic drama with a suggestion of Shakespeare about it; and *Matapan*, by Emile Moreau, a learned and ingenious revival of the kind of burlesque so dear to Théophile Gautier. He was not daunted by the extreme difficulty of staging the dramatic panorama of the French

Revolution, reconstructed from contemporary documents, and called by the Goncourts *La Patrie en Danger*. It is assuredly not fitted for the theatre, and the heroes of the drama look as much like dwarfs straying about on an enormous canvas as the characters in *La Débâcle*. But it was a good thing to give the public and the critics an opportunity of judging it; and after all, even a mere tentative effort of the De Goncourts teaches the world more than a success of Sardou's. The playbill of the Théâtre Libre sometimes on one and the same evening included a comedy in the style of Musset, a fantasy *à la* Banville, and a historical play, such as *La Mort du Duc d'Anguien*, by Léon Hennique. In face of a menu so varied and, one may even say, so appetising, critics forgot the fury which had been roused by the *fumisteries lugubres* of M. Jullien and M. Alexis, and allowed themselves to be appeased. They were even forced to admit that, but for Antoine, they would often have found it difficult to fill their weekly column. The recognised theatres were eternally playing the same pieces and stereotyping pretended successes.

"There is really only one theatre in Paris at this moment," says M. Faguet, who will hardly be suspected of a weakness for innovations, "and it is the Théâtre Libre." This pronouncement justifies the importance that I have felt constrained to assign to M. Antoine.

I have mentioned the psychological school. The most gifted and interesting writer which it brought to light was François de Curel, whose very name seems to indicate an old family with many provincial links. His work, as it proceeds, suggests a proud, concentrated, rather wild nature, which had spent the decisive moments of its youth partly in some solitary corner amongst primitive folk, and partly in some circle of extreme intellectual refinement in Paris. Such a contrast produces a complicated and bizarre moral nature, exceedingly difficult to decipher, and an intellectual development remarkable for its harsh and bitter, almost evil, character, the more alarming in its recklessness and violence for the very restraint and coolness which it preserves. There may, perhaps, be a foundation still more deeply laid; M. de Curel may, perhaps, hide his sensitiveness beneath his irony, just as he hides his irony under the subtle and delicate correctness of his style. If he ever rises to a height of greatness which gives the public a right to demand his self-revelation, and if he can succeed in gratifying them without making himself ridiculous, his will be a curious mind to study.

Les Fossiles was played in November, 1892, at the Théâtre Libre, a sombre play with never a smile in it. Death hovers ceaselessly over it and finally makes its presence felt in the most mournful and solemn fashion, for the fifth act is played around a corpse like the first act of *Richard III.* In its own fashion it asks and answers the same question as that cheerful comedy *Le Gendre de M. Poirier :* what is to become of the old noblesse, and what part can it play in our modern social order ? After half a century of democracy, including twenty years of Republican government, such a question still needed, and still needs, to be asked. I have already pointed out some of the reasons which gave it actuality.

The Duc de Chantemelle, who has passed his
life in his own estates seducing peasant girls and
killing boars, has but one idea in his brain and
one single article in his moral and religious creed
—pride of race. The idea has been transmitted
to his son Robert and his daughter Claire, but
in an idealised form.   Claire breathes into it all
the passionate sorrow of a soul that has never met
with love and is pining away in solitude ; Robert
interprets it with the delicate generosity and
prophetic insight of a mind open to all the needs
of the modern world. To him the nobility is
sacrifice: let the old aristocracy resume the
career of self-devotion, and it will again become
worthy to lead society. Thus to all three natures,
although for different reasons, the highest and
most imperative duty is to perpetuate the race
of Chantemelle. With the father it is sheer
unreasoning pride : he is a solid block of
prejudice almost imposing in its massive simplicity, at any rate in the eyes of those who
think a dolmen more beautiful than a Greek
temple. With the daughter it becomes a worship
of the past, with the son a tender looking forward

to the future. Unhappily, Robert is a prey to a mortal disease, and with him the race will become extinct. But he has had a child by his sister's companion, and he confides the episode to his mother, simply with the idea of securing his mistress's welfare, not of making reparation for his fault. That is one of the cruel, though perhaps legitimate, strokes whereby M. de Curel shows us the difference between a romantic dreamer and an honest man. What use will the Duchess make of this confidence? It gives her a secret and profound shock of pleasure : she had thought Hélène her husband's mistress. Alas! we, the audience, know that her fear was not groundless, and that the Duke had indeed been Hélène's earliest seducer. So that the child—well, in any case, the child is a Chantemelle, and the Duke, instead of being overwhelmed by a sense of his guilt, draws himself up and ordains that Robert shall marry Hélène, and the name be perpetuated. Claire, who knows the frightful secret, Claire, with all her purity and nobility, accepts this infamous solution. When an accident reveals all to Robert, he dies of the blow, but only after ratifying his father's act and regulating its remotest consequences in a will and testament inspired by the most grandiose and chimeric dreams. The Duchess submits in her turn, and before the mystery of death, between the bier of Robert and the cradle of the last of the Chantemelles, the whole family become reconciled; they kneel around their chief, who strikes almost a pontifical attitude. Claire's untiring guardianship will force Hélène to fulfil her duty to the child, the last hope of the race.

The play is vigorous and closely knit; it has its poignant moments, and, in spite of the repulsiveness of its subject, it is not without a certain austere grandeur. Once in the third act, when there is a pause in the action, we are somewhat astonished at coming across a lyrical passage. The world of the sea, peopled by the labouring waves, which rise up, find their own level, and sink away without a moment's pause, symbolises democracy; the forest plunging its roots into the soil and rearing its branches ever higher towards heaven is the heaped-up mass of accumulated life, the shadowy silence of the immovable tradition of the ages—in one word, the aristocracy. Whether in keeping or not, this is a remarkable passage.

L'Envers d'une Sainte is another of M. de Curel's plays, also played at the Théâtre Libre, in which the heroine, Julie Renaudin, loves a man who returns her love, but forgets her and marries another girl. Julie revenges herself by causing the young wife to fall from a plank into a ravine. Jeanne is lifted up dying : she divines the truth, and calling her rival to her bedside forgives everything. She does not die, but she gives birth prematurely to a little girl, and, as the result of this accident, she cannot a second time become a mother. Julie takes the veil, and for more than twenty years teaches in the school of the Sacré Cœur at Vannes. All the world praises her piety and goodness ; she is known as "la sainte." In reality, the convent takes the place of the prison which she had so richly deserved. Henri dies ; and Julie gets released from her vows and returns to the world. She will hardly feel the change, for the pious household kept by her mother and aunt is a sort of sisterhood where the talk is all of " good works " and of " offices." She arrives calm, cold, smiling, joyless, emotionless, into the midst of the tender fluttering attentions of the old women. She meets Jeanne again. Jeanne is a good and simple soul, who desires to be Julie's friend, and admires the beauty and sustained perseverance of her long penitence. Perhaps, too, she is attracted to her by the common bond of their love for the same person. Why should they not talk together of their memories of Henri ? Why not mingle their tears ? But Julie only wishes to know if Henri " thought of her." Jeanne replies very frankly, " Yes, at first." The ghost of Julie was for ever rising between her and her husband'. Then she told him all, the abortive crime and its consequences. Julie imagines that from that moment Henri cursed her memory. A portrait of her, found at the bottom of a fountain, and doubtless thrown there by him, finally convinces her that the man she loved died hating her. Hence her second crime. To avenge herself on Jeanne, she will take Christine away from her mother by breaking off the marriage arranged for her, and impelling her towards a religious life. And the crime would have been accomplished had not Christine's *fiancé* and Jeanne herself fought vigorously against it, and the girl herself been awakened from her momentary hypnotism. The fury of the pretended saint is only appeased, however, when she learns that the thought of her had been cherished by Henri to the last, and that the portrait, which had been the chief cause of her mistake, had been thrown into the fountain by Jeanne herself in a fit of passionate jealousy. Then and only then she humbles herself, as the proud in spirit do humble themselves, sustained by the certainty of having conquered. She returns to the convent, but hers is not the nature that will ever there find true repentance. The word hypocrisy is only once breathed throughout the play, and truly there is no question here of hypocrisy. Julie Renaudin is no hypocrite; she is a violent and passionate soul fully conscious of its own impulses, and showing an alarming degree of moral shamelessness when she reveals herself in her conversations with Aunt Noémi. Of sighs, devout intonations, flat and pious phrases, not a trace. If the damned talk religion, their talk must be like hers.

The setting of the play is that clerical *milieu* which Balzac had already painted in exaggerated colours, a world of gentle, innocent, narrow-minded folk, an atmosphere of exhausted per-fumes and faded colours, a sort of spiritual *potpourri* of sanctity, much inferior to the holiness which blossoms under the free air of heaven, but with a scent and a charm of its own. Here and there, especially in the third act, there are strange circumstantial passages, almost like confidences, which give us to understand that the religious life is an artificial life, a wonderful fragile illusion kept going by odd little makeshifts, but inca-pable of withstanding the smallest contact with reality. Yet all these women are angels. M. de Curel, who leaves us in doubt as to his real opinion of the French aristocracy, is equally enigmatical with regard to the religious idea. His view seems to accord with that of many of the men of his time: " Science is true in itself, but it only produces vanity and egotism, often of a monstrous kind. It is impossible to believe in religion, but without it there can be neither goodness, nor virtue, nor happiness."

L'Envers d'une Sainte is one of the best plays that the psychological school has yet produced, and much might reasonably have been expected of its author. But such pieces of his as have been played at the other theatres have not come up to these expectations. " You are a thinker, a writer : such gifts do not pay on the stage. Cheer up, you see things in too gloomy a light. Be frivolous and witty, that is what the public wants, especially in the first act." I could almost put my finger on the idiots who talked to him in that strain. M. de Curel has something better than wit, but wit he has not. Where he meant to be light and pleasant, he only succeeded in being deplorably vulgar. He is nothing if not serious, and if that is forbidden him, he must give up the game. " We are quite too amusing ! " exclaimed the two daughters of Madame de Grécourt in *L'Invitée*, but they make a mistake ; M. de Curel is wholly incapable of drawing girls who are " quite too amusing," he must leave that to Henri Meilhac, Jules Lemaître, and Henri Lavedan.

L'Invitée, La Figurante, L'Amour Brodé were, to my mind, more than disappointing, for they showed the weaknesses and gaps in the work of an artist who had cast a glamour over me in *Les Fossiles* and *L'Envers d'une Sainte.* Of *L'Amour Brodé* I shall say nothing, because I was utterly unable to understand it. *L'Invitée* is a play which starts from an impossibility and does not succeed in arriving anywhere. A wife, who has learned that her husband is deceiving her, leaves his house, and for fifteen years lives far away from France. She thus allows the world in general to think her mad, and her husband to believe her guilty. Her two little girls she leaves behind to be brought up as they can, which is very badly. One fine day she comes back. Out of curiosity ? As a joke ? In answer to an invitation from her husband, who thinks that he has something to forgive, and that it is to his interest to do it ? I don't know; but assuredly it is not maternal feeling which brings her back, for she is perfectly cool, and almost ironical. M. de Curel's is a remarkable philosophy : it sings the praises of atavism and makes light of the tie of blood. In the last scene Madame de Grécourt says to her husband, "You followed your passions and you were unhappy. I refused to gratify mine and I am unhappy." Whence follows the highly original conclusion that, whatever one does, one is unhappy.

La Figurante did not please me any better. A politician wants to marry a young girl who will keep his house and let him keep his mistress. He finds one who accepts the bargain, but does not stick to it. She was ugly to begin with, and her first care is to make herself beautiful. The statesman falls in love with his wife, and his mistress departs with a broken heart, only happily there turns up an aged husband to pick up the pieces. The subject of the play is distinctly unsavoury, and more in harmony with eighteenth-century manners. A writer of that period would have converted it into a lively and impertinent imbroglio, gliding over its uglier features and laying stress on the fact that all comes right in the end. It might have been called *Françoise, ou le Triomphe de la Modestie.* But the modernity of M. de Curel's treatment brings out both the improbability and the unpleasantness of the subject. I have a poor opinion of Republican Ministers, but I don't go so far as to believe that the portfolio of Foreign Affairs can be bandied about by two such absolutely silly women, or that it would occur to any one to offer it to a contemptible fool like Henri de Renneval, who behaves like a perfect simpleton between the mistress that he is weary of and the wife that he adores. The mistress is the one creature that interests me, and she is the only one of the four accomplices who suffers.

I am forced to admit that, besides having no wit, M. de Curel has hardly any imagination, that his observation is seldom accurate, and that his dialogue is neither easy, nor natural, nor lifelike. He is " literary " in the worst sense of the word, for, in matters theatrical, it is worse to write badly than not to write at all. His sole gift is his ability for analysing a given situation comprising three or four persons, and extracting from it the innumerable shades of sentiment, whether simultaneous or successive, which it holds in solution. No emotions by the way, no capricious fancy, no happy thoughts, none of those sudden impulses which reveal life and do away with the necessity of explaining it. I cited *L'Envers d'une Sainte* as one of the best productions of the psychological school; I must now cite *L'Invitée*, *La Figurante*, and *L'Amour Brodé* as examples of the excesses to which this school is prone.

My desire to follow out M. de Curel's development has made me lose sight of the Théâtre Libre; now I come back to it just in time to see it close its doors after a career of more than eight years.   Every one knows that M. Antoine did not make a fortune at the Théâtre Libre.   When he was appointed Director of the Odéon, together with the journalist Paul Ginisty, the Minister said to him, "I accept you, M. Antoine, with all your consequences."   It was a bold and intelligent step.   We thought that the second French theatre would become a glorified and State-supported Théâtre Libre, but for some reason or another the Antoine-Ginisty duumvirate did not last.   After a year's absence M. Antoine reappeared before a Parisian audience at the

Théâtre des Menus Plaisirs, assisted by his former collaborators, led by M. François de Curel and M. Brieux. It was the return from Elba of the dramatic world; may it not culminate in a Waterloo ! But, however this new campaign may turn out, I have proved, I think, the right of the Théâtre Libre to an important place in the evolution of our stage. The brave little theatre has had its day and done its work. Its decisive experience has resulted in the *reductio ad absurdum* of certain theories which will never reappear, and it has sown seeds destined to spring up and flourish in the drama of to-day.

IV.

ROUND ABOUT THE THEATRES.

Eighteen months ago, when I once more began
to haunt the Paris theatres, I found them pretty
much as I had left them five-and-twenty years
back. Indeed, I could only wonder that I was
not more astonished. Can a quarter of a century
really make so little impression upon scenes
frequented nightly by the palpitating, fluctuating life of the most inquisitive and capricious
nation in the world? One felt it even before
one had entered. There were my old friends,
the ticket mongers, ready to lay hands on me
and drag me off to some wretched little café or
wine-shop on the pretext of selling me an
"excellent stall." The transaction, which has
rather a shady look, is carried on on behalf of
the authors, who take this means of selling their
complimentary tickets. If it is an abuse, it

ought to be done away with; if it is a recognised privilege, why not exercise it in a regular and honourable fashion?

But I have fallen into the hands of the *ouvreuses*—I beg their pardon, the *placeuses*. They have changed their name but not their physiognomy or their nature. My coat and hat are snatched away, and will be thrust on to my knees during the last *entr'acte* "to avoid the crowd"; in other words, to levy their tax more conveniently.

Boxes, which are almost a thing of the past in English theatres, are still in favour here, rising three or four deep from the ground floor all round the house. The hot air mounting up makes the top ones unbearable, whilst from the lower ones, which are stuck right down behind the pit, you see the stage much as you might see the sky from the depths of a tunnel. One would be comfortable enough in the stalls, although the incline is less well managed than in England, but for the new feminine craze for large hats. When the two bunches of feathers just in front of me lean confidentially towards each other, they hide the whole stage from the footlights to the flies.

I ask for *l'Entr'acte*, the programme-journal of former days, and am told that it is dead; but in its place I am given an elegant little book tied with green ribbon. It is an excellent advertisement for the paper called *l'Illustration*, and it contains portraits of actors and actresses, with little scraps of biography.

The theatres are still too brilliantly lighted, both in the intervals and during the performance —a custom which mars the scenic effect, and also induces a less collected frame of mind in the spectator. One cannot yet escape seeing the vacant, surly faces of the orchestra, or, if one is in the first row, hearing their silly remarks. The *claque* has migrated to the upper regions, but it still makes its wearisome presence felt. At intervals the heavy, mechanical clap of sixty paid hands swells out and dies away, hailing a *mot*, punctuating a tirade, marking the place where the author thinks he has said a clever thing, or the actor fancies he has made a hit. The public suffer this as patiently as ever;

indeed, their own applause seems to me tardier than when I was young.

It is not strange, when one comes to think of it, that there should have been so little change in the theatrical world, for it is still governed by the same men and animated by the same spirit. The Théâtre Français is ruled by an order signed by Napoleon at the Kremlin in 1812, and known as the Moscow Decree. Here is another fact which ought to convince foreigners that, for all our revolutionary fanfaronades, we are an essentially conservative and routine-loving nation. What a piece of folly it is that men who knew nothing of the stage could force it to conform to their cherished dream of bureau-cratic centralisation. The system is excessively complicated. First the *pensionnaires* engaged on the ordinary conditions, and distinguished from the *sociétaires*, who, in addition to their fixed salary, receive a share in the returns. Then an infinity of grades, ranging from those who receive a twelfth or sixteenth fraction of a share up to those who have a whole share! Partnership ensures a pension, but imposes such stringent conditions that very many artists prefer to sacrifice it all for freedom.

The Comédie Française is often engaged in litigation, worth nothing even when it is successful. Add to that the bitter rivalry between the various grades of that curious artistic hierarchy, with its gradual advance towards seniority and its failure, sometimes, to give talent its due recognition. Such rivalry gives birth to disputes, all the more difficult to settle because modern rôles do not correspond to the older definitions of "parts." Above this aristocracy of the sociétaires there is the oligarchical dictatorship of the Comité de lecture, which, in secret conclave, accepts or rejects the plays submitted to its judgment. Two readers, chosen outside from amongst the most experienced critics and theatrical experts—M. Paul Perret and M. Edouard Carol fill the post for the moment—look through all the manuscripts sent in, and save the valuable time of the Committee by weeding out mad and impossible plays. It need hardly be said that authors already known to the house are spared these preliminaries and come at once before the final judges. Ever since

I was old enough to read newspapers there has been a perpetual running fire of complaints and sarcasms directed against the Reading Committee of the Théâtre Français, from the days of Casimir Delavigne down to M. Emile Bergerat. Above all these lesser people is the Administrator-General, the most wretched and impotent of men unless, like M. Jules Claretie, he retrieves a false situation by prestige, by strength of will, by patience and tact. Such machinery could hardly have been expected to work forty-eight hours; but it has gone on working eighty-five years.

The action of Coquelin and Sarah Bernhardt seems to indicate that the Comédie Française will be hard put to it to retain actors of genius. I am not even sure that it is a paradise for good artists of the second rank; but, on the other hand, third-rate people flourish and grow fat in these prebendal stalls of the drama. They make up for lack of talent by presence and traditions, perhaps a little too much of them. They cannot forget for one moment that they are "the first comedians in the world," but by being too careful to remember it themselves they risk having it forgotten by the audience.

I have already spoken of my admiration for Madame Bartet, though I regret that she is condemned, to perpetual elegiacs. Mdlle. Reichemberg, *la petite doyenne*, is the sole survivor of the days when I had the *entrée* of the Comédie. Then I did not care for her at all, but last winter I thought her charming. How fresh and young her voice is compared with Mdlle. Brandès and Mdlle. Marsy ! I admit that I was disposed to be rather exacting in Mdlle. Marsy's case; I had heard so much of *la belle Marsy*. Moreover, the authors who wrote parts for her seemed to think that her astonishing loveliness would cover all improbabilities and explain every kind of folly. Certainly I thought Mdlle. Marsy beautiful, but utterly lacking in that indefinable quality of magnetism, poetry, charm, with not the very smallest *je ne sais quoi*. How could she love, weep, suffer, say subtle things that touch the soul, be convincing in the part of a young girl? As for Mdlle. Brandès, I shall wait for a better opportunity of judging her. I saw her in one of those twin comediettas which M. Edouard Pailleron united somewhat arbitrarily and fantastically, under the rather incomprehensible title *Mieux vaut Douceur—et Violence.* The moral of the first is that a wife who wants to win back a faithless husband, or a husband on the verge of betraying her, should get into a passion ; whilst the second indicates that she ought to do quite the contrary, and the climax of bewilderment is reached when *Violence* is played first and *Douceur* at the end of the evening. Certainly these two sketches *à la* Vercousin would hardly have secured M. Pailleron's election to the Academy. *Violence* was played by Mdlles. Brandès and Marsy, and between them a young man, M. Dehelly, with now and again an echo of Delaunay's voice, but with a nervous trick of trembling which soon became wearisome. The trio reminded me of some very tolerable provincial theatre in a prefecture of forty thousand souls, where there is a bishop and a Court of Appeal. But the interpretation rose to a distinctly higher level in *Douceur*, thanks to Mdlle. Reichemberg and M. de Féraudy —a charming comedian, a comedian born, in every respect worthy to uphold the traditions of the theatre and to create precedents of his own.

In modern comedy I made acquaintance with M. le Bargy and M. Leloir, who seemed very intelligent actors, but I could not discover in them any note of originality. Perhaps that was the fault of their parts. M. le Bargy is apparently "the man of the world," as Bressaut was thirty-five years ago. Only Bressaut created a type worthy of the careful study of the gentlemen of his time ; M. le Bargy merely reproduces, with marvellous exactness, the dominant type.

I would rather say nothing about a great artist like Mounet Sully, seeing that any praise which I could offer, after an incomplete study of his great gifts, must necessarily fall far short of his deserts. Every one combined to assure me that he was admirable, that it was a pure joy to see and hear him in the great parts, into which he pours his whole soul. It seemed to me that the almost identical treatment of classical tragedy and romantic drama at the Théâtre Français tended to bring the two closer together. Once they had totally opposite traditions, but in time they will be united. The same artists play *Phèdre* and *Ruy Blas* very nearly in the same fashion. They think that they do well in breathing a little life and human feeling into the cold marble of classical drama. But they are wrong. Tragedy has a life of its own, and a special form of sensibility which needs a special mode of utterance. Leave it as it is, it is an insult to modernise it; to infect it with our modern life is a sure means of killing it. You do not ask of a statue that warm blood should flow in its veins. *Sint ut sunt, aut non sint.*

I spent a Sunday afternoon at the Théâtre Français, and saw *L'Avare* and *Monsieur de Pourceaugnac.* Coquelin *cadet* was Pourceaugnac. I need hardly say that he acted like the excellent comedian that he is, but without exerting himself. M. Laugier, as Harpagon, did not remind me either of Provost or Talbot, both of whom I have seen in the part. He has none of the spontaneity and originality of the first, but he is much less lugubrious and much more master of himself than the second, who appears to have thought Harpagon an alarming personage to be painted in the darkest colours. M. Truffier played Maître Jacques and Sbrigani very conscientiously. The Nérine and Frosine of Mdlle. Kalb and Mdlle. Fayolle showed, or rather suggested, that the traditions of Augustine Brohan have not yet quite fallen into oblivion. Some very good actors played quite small parts; M. Laugier was the first doctor, and M. de Féraudy drawled out the thirty lines which constitute the apothecary's part. This admirable custom, which prevails nowhere else, is the greatest mark of respect that can be paid to the masters of dramatic literature, and is one of the most effective ways of maintaining the art of interpretation at a high level.

The *matassins*, with their instruments, were there in full force, and pursued M. de Pourceaugnac with no great air of conviction as far as I could see, but with all the proper solemnities. They passed down into the house, and all trod on my toes as they ran through the orchestra —their foolish heads peeping through the prompter's box and suddenly withdrawn to dodge the blows which echo through the house, the fat man disguised in woman's clothes, the grotesque dancers kicking up their heels to their nightcaps, were all terribly like a pantomime at the Folies-Bergère. Nothing was wanting but the Hanlon-Lees.

Moreover, it was a regular Folies-Bergère audience. Two monkey-faced Brazilians sitting beside me were humming and munching all the time. Three Germans behind me were following the play with a book. The wise and witty utterances fell perfectly flat; but the horseplay was greeted with never-ending peals of childish laughter. When Harpagon exclaimed "I would rather see my daughter dead!" there was a little murmur of protestation which entertained me vastly, and set me thinking as to whether I had any right to laugh at these good people. Why should they not think that Harpagon was going a little too far? If we had not been taken quite young and made to swallow all these phrases at an age when one can digest anything—if we looked at *L'Avare* with as open a mind and as unbiassed a judgment as we bring to the consideration of new plays, might we not very well say, "Here is a pupil of

M. Becque's, much cleverer than his master, but ready to exaggerate all his audacities? This father, who would rather see his daughter dead than give her a dowry; these children, conspiring to rob and deceive their father and to set him at defiance; surely they all belong to the *comédie rosse*, and *rosse* with a vengeance! Here is a drama which takes more liberties than the Théâtre Libre!" As for the monologue about the stolen casket, which has been translated almost word for word from Plautus, sincerity would compel us to admit that it is as bad as it can possibly be, and that there is not one touch of brightness or naturalness in the whole scene.

The Odéon, like the Comédie Française, is a subsidised theatre, but unaffected by the famous decree of Moscow. Governmental interference confines itself to nominating the manager, and now and again granting an "ordre de début" to some young *tragédienne* who has friends in official circles. Further, two nights a week must be reserved for old-established plays and for the productions of new writers; so that the subscribers can reckon upon a varied bill. I thought the Odéon very prosperous and full of life, altogether different from what it was in my youth. In those days no one ever went there except on great occasions, such as the first night of *Gaëtana.* Parisians living on the right bank of the river spoke of the Odéon as a somewhat unknown and badly-lighted place. So it was; there was a mournful sound even about the applause as it echoed through an empty and melancholy house. A generation earlier things were even worse. Nadaud makes the *étudiante* in his *Lettre à l'Etudiant* say—

> "Et l'on joua la pauvre pièce
> Devant trois polytechniciens,
> Treize claqueurs, une négresse
> Et puis nous deux, tu t'en souviens."

The times have changed. I saw one of Marivaux' plays rattled off most vigorously by a very intelligent company. I saw Jean Richepin's *Le Chemineau* admirably played to a crowded and enthusiastic house. I had not the pleasure of applauding Mdlle. Tessandier, but I was much struck by Madame Segond Weber.

Having only seen her once, I cannot of course tell how far she can vary her effects. Her voice that evening was rough and tired, and if that is its normal condition, her artistic gifts must suffer some limitation. But her dramatic perception is both pure and powerful; she is sincere, she is human, she stirs some secret spring in us, and she is more capable of achieving something great than any other contemporary French actress except Sarah Bernhardt. But apart from that, the Odéon is doing well. What with its modern nights and its classical nights, its legion of brilliant lecturers, and the marked favour shown to it by the academic world, which is both more numerous, more active, and more influential than it used to be, it has a brilliant future before it.

Unlike the London theatres, which are almost all in the hands of actor-managers, who monopolise their own stage and order a part as if they were ordering a coat, we have quite a large assortment of different kinds of managers. One is a journalist with ideas; another an actor, but an actor who has ceased to act; a third an author who has by no means ceased to write but whose plays are played by his neighbours; a fourth is a man of business whose name suggests that his ancestors inhabited the Holy Land before the destruction of the Temple. We have also a manager whose wife acts, though he does not act himself. And, finally, the actor-manager is worthily represented, as all will agree, by Coquelin and Sarah Bernhardt. I do not know whether Sarah Bernhardt has made money at the Renaissance, but I know that she has done good service to the cause of art. As to Coquelin he has already reigned several years at the Porte Saint Martin, and he ended his dramatic season in 1897, with a hundred representations of *Colonel Roquebrune,* when he made his audience shout *Vive l'Empereur* as fervently as they shouted *Vive le Roi* to his Duguesclin. When he is playing George Ohnet or Déroulède before a Porte Saint Martin audience, one loses a few of the finer shades, but on the other hand the actor's talent grows, his voice acquires new vibrations irresistible in their resonance and emotional power. What tragic force lay hidden in the comedian of old days, and with what a commanding touch he now sweeps the whole gamut of emotion !

In one of the intervals of *Colonel Roquebrune* we knocked at the glass door which opens out of the public greenroom on to a private staircase. It opened, and in a few moments we were in Coquelin's dressing-room—a very light room, soberly furnished, but in excellent taste, containing a table strewn with papers and a large white marble toilet apparatus. The man himself is so simple and genial, so straightforward and open-handed ; his words are as ready as his thought is quick. An obliging guest showed him some autographs, a medal struck in 1870, and a few other antique and modern curiosities which he examined like a connoisseur. Then the talk drifted to the stage, and the way in which he pulled a play to pieces and reconstructed it in five minutes showed me that in such a manager and such an interpreter a dramatic author would find an invaluable collaborator. No one ever gave me a stronger impression of a great artist than Coquelin that evening. I felt as if I were talking, not to a contemporary, but to the ghost of Kean or Talma called back by magic from the spirit world. Twice a message was brought to him, " Monsieur, may we begin ? " "Directly, directly," and Coquelin resumed his discourse with a freedom of gesture and a tone of conviction. At last the house got restive, we took our leave, and the actor shook hands with us as he put on his Colonel's uniform. I had hardly got back to the house before I heard his magnificent voice thundering on the stage.

I spoke just now of the Renaissance, the elegant theatre given up to the operettas of Strauss and Lecocq, before the reign of Sarah Bernhardt. In those days people went there to applaud Mdlle. Jeanne Granier; they still go to applaud her, but in a different capacity. Then she sang, now she acts. The former diva of operetta has come out as a comedian. The *Avatar* of Madame Judic's dreams has been realised by Jeanne Granier. She has appeared as Claudine Rozay, the heroine of a piece called *Amants*, by M. Donnay, which I shall have occasion to speak of later on. It reveals a section of the *demi monde* undealt with by Dumas, the *demi monde* bourgeois, into which his Baronne d'Ange never entered. The *comédienne* contributed much to the success of the play, and the author recognised this by dedicating it to her. With her pretty, caressing ways, and her enchanting little air of maternal wisdom towards her lover, Jeanne Granier proved the best possible interpreter of those delicate sensual natures, sweet and tender even in their infidelity, adroit and prudent even in the abandonment and exaltation of love. To these women passion is no enduring condition, but a critical moment. When the moment is past they are safe, they and all that surrounds them. Mdlle. Granier has identified herself with this purely Parisian type of character.

If we look in at the Palais Royal we shall find Mdlle. Lavigne as triumphantly successful as ever. She is "Lavigne" to the *habitués* of the theatre—a familiarity which means glory. Whether politician, poet, or artist, a man only becomes a somebody when he ceases to be

Monsieur. Lavigne, then, has created a new type of feminine character, the pretty grotesque. These things can't be explained, one must go and see them, and go too without loss of time. For, in all human probability, Mdlle. Lavigne will cease to be pretty long before she ceases to be grotesque, and then we shall only have an excellent duenna, such as we had once in Thierret and Boisgoutier.

The Vaudeville and the Gymnase are united under the same management, but I do not think that the inventors of that combination have much to be proud of. Since the combined companies only contain one artist calculated to draw, Madame Réjane, to make a proper use of her power of attracting audiences the management ought to commission a young author with no false prejudices to write plays so arranged that the artist could, on one and the same evening, run from the Chaussée d'Antin to the Boulevart Bonne Nouvelle, and appear in the first act at one theatre, in the second at the other, and so on, without either piece suffering unduly from her momentary eclipse. Will the managers try the experiment? I make them a present of the suggestion. In the actual state of the case one of the two theatres flourishes, whilst the other vegetates. This reminds one of the fate of the Siamese twins, when one of them fell ill and seemed likely to die. And the dénouement will be the same in both cases—amputation.

The unquestionable beauty of Madame Jane Hading does not suffice to draw an audience to a theatre which remembers Rose Cheri, Victoria Lafontaine, and Aimée Desclée, and which was taught only yesterday by Madame Pasca what is really meant by a lady. There are gifts which remain at a provincial level even after twenty years of Paris.

At the Vaudeville, Réjane makes bad plays good, and turns all the lead that is brought her into gold. I only saw her three times—in *Madame Sans-Gêne, Lysistrata,* and *La Doulour-euse,* but that was enough to assure me of her popularity. When she came on the stage the house woke up and the scene brightened just as if the footlights had been turned up. Where does she get that power, that intimate sympathy, that perfect understanding with her audience, which makes her able to convulse them by a mere wink or an "Ahem"? Is it her beauty? Certainly not. She is not pretty, one might even say . . . but it is more polite not to say it. To quote a famous *mot*, "she is not beautiful, she is worse." Her queer little face catches hold of you, by both the good and bad elements in your nature. All the intelligence, the devotion, the pity of a woman are to be read in her wonderful eyes, but below there is the nose and mouth of a sensual little creature, a vicious, almost vulgar, smile, lips pouted for a kiss, but with a lingering, or a dawning, suggestion of irony. Moreover, she is exactly the reigning type, the type that one meets constantly on the Paris pavements when the shop girls are going to lunch. If you happen to be born marquise or duchesse you copy the type, and the result is all the more piquant.

Has Réjane a temperament of her own, a nature peculiar to herself, or is she just a monkey with an incomparable power of imitating every sort of character? If I shut my eyes I some-times think I can hear the nasal intonation, the little squeaky voice which belonged to Céline Chaumont. A minute later this voice has the cadence, the sustained vibration, the artistic break, with which Sarah Bernhardt punctuates her diction, and the transition is so skilfully managed that all these different women—the woman who mocks, the woman who trembles, the woman who threatens, the woman who desires, the woman who laughs, and the woman who weeps—seem to be one and the same woman. For the matter of that I have set myself a problem which I should not be able to solve even with the help of Réjane herself. Let us be content with what lies on the surface. I am inclined to think that her resources consist of a host of petty artifices, each more ingenious and more imperceptible than the last. If one studied her secret one might draw up a whole set of rules for the use of *comédiennes*.

These little profile drawings of artists give a very fair idea of the figures that one may expect on the second plane. I used in old days to go to the *Ecole Lyrique*, in the Rue de la Tour d'Auvergne, which was managed by Ricour. This good fellow, who boasted that he had endowed France with many great artists, had certain invariable methods of discovering and classifying vocations. He ranged the *nez-retroussés* on his right, the Greek and Roman noses on his left. He made the first lot pronounce a word which he had invented, "éléganté," and the second lot a word, also of his own invention, "superbatandor." It was the masonic test according to which he gave his decision. "My child, *you* are a *tragédienne*, and *you* will play comedy." If poor Ricour were to come back to the world he would have to change his test. There is now a kind of drama suited to the *nez-retroussés*, that is to say, for those who cannot say "superbatandor," only it is passion transposed into another key. The difference consists chiefly in the social *milieu* and physical characteristics. After testing their qualifications, a modern Ricour would probably say to his pupils, "*You* will be a mistress in the grand style, a cosmopolitan great lady, and *you* a bourgeoise of the Boulevard Malesherbes with a lover." They would not listen, and each would choose a model for herself amongst the queens of the theatre. The Conservatoire, which is the ante-chamber and nursery of the theatrical world, is full of would-be Bartets, Réjanes in embryo, and Sarahs in miniature. An actress' talent is often simply a question of fantastic dilettantism or of chic. She aims at originality instead of studying nature, and every day gets a little further off from the real sincerity which fascinated us in Desclée, and which makes the acting of Eleonora Duse so touching.

The prevailing type amongst actors indicates the change which has taken place in the national manners. One feels that all the world has gone through the conscription. Little turned - up waxed moustaches, closely cropped hair brushed backwards, well-fitting clothes, head up, chin in the air, eyes looking haughtily down from under lowered eyelids, and a stiff soldierly gait, are apparently the qualifications needed in a beloved object. All this militarism is nevertheless only a matter of externals, with no effect upon diction or ideas. For the matter of that these lady killers have not, at first sight, anything very seductive about them. Lafont, Bressaut, Berton père, Delaunay, took endless trouble to justify the mad things that were done for their sake. Now, apparently, the love of women for men does not need any explanation. Men are loved because fate wills it so. They are not handsome, they do not seek to please, they have no soft tones in their voice, no caressing looks. They are men, that is enough. I do not regret the jeune premier, that stupid and tiresome personage who, for two hundred years, has dragged out a weary existence in all our plays and comedies. However, there are still men who are lovers by character and by profession. Such, for example, is Sir George Lamorant, Mr. Pinero's Butterfly, so well acted by Mr. George Alexander. During my voyage of discovery amongst the Parisian theatres I did not meet with one single actor who appeared to be made for these parts, or who had any idea of training himself for them. That state of things will continue throughout the reign of the new psychology which I have already spoken of in connection with the Théâtre Libre, and which makes Don Juan a domestic dupe, a subject for feminine exploitation.

I think that we can now pretty well appreciate the situation of the younger dramatic writers, the matter with which they have to deal, the difficulties that they will encounter, and the resources at their disposal. On the one hand you have a theatrical world which has hardly changed for five-and-twenty years, artists brought up in old traditions, managers who want to make money, and who think that for this purpose old recipes are safer than modern tendencies. Their public is somewhat contemptuous, sleepy, indifferent, both philistine and blasé ; it comes to the theatre now, as of old, to be amused, to have its feelings stirred, and, above all, to have its senses titillated. This public has to be lured away from feats of horsemanship, American gymnasts, Japanese jugglers, Italian clowns, women who eat fire or smoke under water, or dance on a rainbow, or twist their bodies about like a piece of live indiarubber—in short, from all the eccentricities and immodesties of the circus and of the music hall. But, for all that, this public has its moments of sentimental weakness and its sudden outbursts of morality. On the other side stands a little group, small in number, but eager to make its voice heard, and pushing the world on without knowing exactly where it is going, or what it wants, or what it thinks, except that Dumas and Augier are blockheads, and that their theatre is quite antediluvian. This group has turned in succession towards naturalism, symbolism, and pure psychology. It has sought salvation in Henry Becque, in Maeterlinck, and in Ibsen—everywhere rather than in Dumas; and whilst it goes on shouting its reiterated anathemas in all the literary societies, in all the offices of the little unreadable reviews, in the artists' cafés of Montmartre and of the Boulevard Saint Michel, the managers whisper in the ears of the authors: "Give us something like the work of Dumas fils, or, if you can, Dumas père; that would be better still for our pockets." Assuredly, I say again, the position of dramatic authors is not enviable.

What is criticism doing to help us? Dramatic

criticism in Paris is a very numerous, very complicated, and very flourishing hierarchy. At the head of it stand those grave and reverend signors, the Monday *feuilletonistes*. They have often several days to reflect in before giving their decision. It is only on Sunday evening that the printer expects their twelve columns, which are often far too narrow for the variety and importance of the matters demanding treatment. But after the full weeks come the weeks of leanness. Sometimes there is nothing to fill up the twelve columns with but a farce at the Théâtre Déjazet, and sometimes nothing at all. In the summer, between the Fair of Neuilly and the re-opening of the Odéon, there are some terrible months to get through. At moments like these M. Jules Lemaître, when he was critic of the *Débats*, sat down courageously to re-read his " Lamartine " and to give us his impressions of it. Another time he set himself a little problem and worked out several solutions, each contradicting the last, as is the habit of his subtle mind. The question was, who could have seduced Marceline Desbordes-Valmore, a young actress born at Douai towards the end of the last century, who wrote bad verses in her maturer years, and who has recently had a statue erected to her, much to her injury, as if we were overstocked with marble for chimney-pieces or bronze to make pennies with! M. Emile Faguet never wrote so charming a theatrical criticism as on a certain day when he had absolutely nothing to say.

These elegant exercises, however, are not suited to all the world. They need a certain grace, a command of literary artifices, a readiness and subtlety of mind which few writers possess: and, to be quite frank, it is perhaps not to be desired that this art of talking, and talking so well, for the sake of saying nothing should make further progress amongst us. There is something just a little bit absurd, when one comes to think of it, in this weekly *feuilleton*, with its enormous variation in matter and its utter absence of variation in dimensions. Besides, papers which pride themselves on actuality cannot make their readers wait an entire week, for the account of a *première*. That is why the *Figaro*, the *Gaulois*, the *Journal*, and all the papers which make literary and fashionable news more prominent than political dissertations, publish their critical article on the day after the representation. The reader opens his paper, whilst his coffee or his chocolate is getting cold, and finds the account of the play only six or seven hours after the curtain has fallen on the last scene. He likes to imagine the devoted critic perspiring over his nocturnal task and feverishly covering page after page, to be carried off still wet by the printer's devil. But about that there is a little illusion. The critic generally writes his account of the first night twenty-four hours before it takes place, as he leaves the dress rehearsal. If the subject has already been treated by a French or foreign writer, an hour spent at the National Library will be very useful to *corser* the article. At a pinch, if one is not very fastidious, and if one is writing for people who are still less so, one contents oneself with turning over the pages of the editorial *Larousse.* Given imagination and wit, there are other resources still. M. Catulle Mendès, for example, one evening last winter had to tell the public the story of Jean Richepin's *Le Chemineau.* Le Chemineau is the eternal vagabond, the incorrigible wanderer whom nothing can keep in one place, and nothing can steady—neither interest, nor love, nor paternity, not even happiness—and who in the end will take to the road again until he falls and dies in a ditch. Ah! what a mysterious attraction that high road exercises over the hearts and imaginations of men! Many are slaves to it all their lives; all have felt its power, and yielded to its influence in their youth, and here we have M. Catulle Mendès arraigning the high road, questioning it, making it yield up the secret of its strange power. The article is charming, and I am far from complaining of it, but it is clear that that page was written beforehand. We brethren of the pen can recognise each other in our writings, just as masons recognise each other in bricks and plaster. I have made a close examination of a critical article signed by a well-known name. I find 133 lines dating from the day before and $14\frac{1}{2}$ which might have been written on leaving the theatre. Hence it follows that if the Monday criticisms are a trifle stale, the others are certainly a little "previous." I have paid no attention to the "Soiriste," to "Monsieur de l'Orchestre," or to all the host of literary hacks and reporters who have to describe the scenery and dresses, and to gather up for the public the gossip of the greenroom and the corridors. All these people follow close on the heels—sometimes tread on the toes—of criticism, which is so much taken up with defending itself against them that it almost forgets to pursue its own trade.

Clearly this has nothing to do with the masters of the *feuilleton.* At their head stands our excellent Francisque Sarcey, whom we call "cher maître" and, more familiarly still, "mon oncle." Englishmen will understand quite well what that name means. It implies a sort of paternity, more indulgent but, at the same time, more clear-sighted, without responsibility, but also without illusions. Uncle Sarcey has no passionate prejudices, only a few harmless manias which are very well known in Paris, and which give great amusement. If Sarcey's "Dadas" came to an end, there would be a sensible blank in Parisian conversation. He has his own ideas with regard to the chief problems of dramatic art, and his own view of every kind of style, every author and artist. He has his views as to the proper hour for beginning, and the price of places, and on all these questions, big and little, he is in the habit of going straight ahead to his solution. Dumas, who recognised in him both his adversary and his friend, foreseeing, perhaps, that his literary memory would have no better defender, had the justice to say of him that " he always gives his impressions resolutely and frankly, even when they are contradictory." This perfect indepen-dence, this absolute honesty which cannot be moved an inch by the warmest and best-founded personal sympathy, and which is untouched by any consideration of vanity, kindliness, or self-interest, is the dominant and most characteristic quality of Francisque Sarcey. Add to that a wide culture strengthened by forty years of study and experience, and an easy natural wit bubbling up spontaneously both in speech and writing. Moreover, he has remained one of the public, even one of the well-disposed public. Wonderful to relate he is still a lover of the theatre, in spite of the number of evenings that he has spent there. He may have seen some farce of Bisson's ten times, and yet the tenth time "he shakes with laughter in his corner." Another evening it is a melodrama "which goes straight to his heart." To have impressions and the power of expressing them seems quite a simple thing; nevertheless there are very few men capable of it.

Sarcey, in his literary and somewhat bourgeois fashion, represents the good sense and logic which has made the fortune of French wit, but which nowadays is, perhaps, something of an obstacle to its growth and development. He is full of good-will and sincere desire to understand and welcome newcomers; but "the well-constructed play" is bone of his bone, and flesh of his flesh; it has become, in his case, second nature. His one test is logical sequence, and in spite of himself he comes back to that even when he wishes, and intends, to employ another. If he were pressed to give it up, he might reply, like Choppart in the *Courrier de Lyon*, "It is my head that you are asking me for." Even if Sarcey, in an excess of good-will and kindliness, were disposed to make the sacrifice, I hope that no one would be imprudent, or cruel, enough to accept it.

M. Sarcey makes his personality felt by the outspokenness and energy of his convictions. M. Lemaître has won his way by the subtle irony and graceful ease of his scepticism. He interrupts himself now and again to say, " Really I almost meant that " ; and sometimes, when he comes to the end of his reasoning, and is within an inch of concluding, he overturns his argument with a stroke, and decides that perhaps the very opposite is really true. He has a secret for making this sort of pastime attractive—a secret which is his very own, for he made his would-be imitators repent of their temerity.

Only once has he shown himself violent and positive—when he was bent on the slaughter of M. George Ohnet. M. Ohnet was making capital progress towards becoming a great writer. He had just got into the Revue des Deux Mondes, and he was on the high road to the Academy. But, in the nick of time, M. Lemaître cried, " Who goes there ? " and charged and defeated the enemy.

Doubtless it is well from time to time to be reminded that notoriety is not fame, and that all printed paper is not literature ; but was it really worth while to put a cord into M. George Ohnet's hands and to tell him to hang himself before the statue of Flaubert ? If M. Lemaître wanted a bit of hangman's rope, could he not with all his resources have found some other means of procuring the desired talisman ? Moreover, M. Ohnet did not hang himself, though, if he had done it, he could not have been more dead to literature ; there is less life in him now than in many actual corpses. It is a terrible proof of the power exercised by Lemaître at a given moment over the public in general and the younger generation in particular. He showed it in another and less edifying instance. He demolished Renan and set him on his legs again in three days—a charming amusement but a dangerous example. Who knows whether at this moment there is not some little boy playing ball in the Luxembourg Gardens, who in his turn will demolish M. Lemaître ? It would not be so very difficult, for he is by no means cut all in one piece, and the bits are not very closely fitted. Besides, who would put him together again?

His successor on the *Débats*, M. Emile Faguet, is a man of a very different temperament. He is a most fertile writer with his eye everywhere and his finger in everything. He makes nothing of taking the measure of a man, disentangling the leading idea of a play, and constructing or overturning a dramatic system. I am always a little staggered by the honesty of conjurers, and it would in no way surprise me if M. Faguet, with his marvellous intellectual dexterity, were tempted to be a bit of a sophist. But no, he is the very impersonation of good faith. He makes every effort to understand the ideas of the younger writers so as to instil a little method and unity and intelligence into their productions. He makes loyal objections and accepts them with his characteristic phrase: " I am quite ready, for my part. You know that in art I welcome whatever is offered to me provided that it succeeds." It is a very wide formula, but not without a suspicion of some ironical *arrière pensée*, like M. Brunetière's advice to the symbolists, " Gentlemen, pray produce masterpieces." Will the younger generation accept M. Faguet as their spiritual director ? I wish they may, but I am a little uncertain. Possibly they are a little afraid that even he retains a certain habit of mind stronger even than his good-will. To put it shortly, his gown is a little disquieting. M. Faguet is a professor.

Sarcey, Lemaître, Faguet—three professors ! They betray themselves, not by pedantry—they have not a shadow of it—but by their worship of time-honoured models, and by the unwearying zeal with which they always go back to the works of the masters of the seventeenth century when they want instances to point their morals. Are there no critics, then, who are not professors ? Of course there are, but even they seek their ideal in the past. They are as confirmed Shakespeareans or Hugolaters as the others are Racinians and Molièristes. In short, there are two sorts of *vieux jeu*, the romantic and the classic, and neither can guide young authors towards a new form of art.

My account of theatrical criticism would be incomplete if I said nothing about oral criticism, which flourishes everywhere, but more especially

at the Bodinière and at the Classical Thursdays
of the Odéon. This Bodinière is a long room, opening out of a still longer gallery, and affording a
favourable field for conversation. All Paris has
passed through it. It makes trial of men, ideas,
styles, systems ; people play, harangue, sing—
sometimes all three together—and it is no unusual
thing to see a lecturer in a black coat escorted by
a pretty little artist, a sort of living vignette to
his text. At the Bodinière strength wastes itself
in all directions, but at the Odéon it has for ten
years been patiently and intelligently directed to
the revival of forgotten works—a sort of literary
taking stock of the riches of our earlier drama.
More than a hundred plays have already been
resuscitated, each accompanied by an explanatory
lecture reconstructing the *milieu* in which it was
produced, defining and classifying it, and up to a
certain point passing judgment on it, but with
all due deference to the public as the judge in
the last resort. MM. Sarcey, Lemaître, Brunetière, and Chantavoine led the way, and they
have been followed by a whole generation of
young orators. On the day when I went to

the Odéon M. Eugène Lintilhac was lecturing, and the play selected was Marivaux' *Le Prince Travesti.* The audience was very unlike what I had found at the matinée of the Français. It was an audience of *habitués*, very lively and talkative ; a murmur of conversation rose from the boxes, the orchestra was packed with actresses and blue stockings, and the pit was full of students and schoolboys, both literary and mischievous. Exactly at half-past one they began shouting for the lecturer by his Christian name, "Eugène, Eugène!" The curtain rose and Eugène appeared. He gave us an elegant discourse, well arranged, full of matter, agreeably delivered, and just of the right oratorical warmth, neither too hot nor too cold. It was important to make us anxious to see the play, but it was also important to prove that Eugène was not stupid, and that he knew very well where his author's shoe pinched. Marivaux is an unrivalled delineator of the dawn of love. Once and once only, in *Le Prince Travesti,* he tried to paint love in its maturity, with its tears, its struggles, its storms; he slipped from idyl into melodrama. But it was a mistake, and a mistake which explains why the play was consigned to oblivion, and why it will return there to-morrow. Away with it for a century !

I am surprised that no English manager has yet thought of transferring these classical matinées to London, and reviving three centuries of the stage, from *Gorboduc* and *Gammer Gurton's Needle* to the comedies of Douglas Jerrold. Certainly, neither artists, nor lecturers, nor the public, would fail to answer to the call. It would be delightful.

It would be delightful, but it would be no use counting on it to mould or ripen the drama of to-morrow. There is nothing for young authors to learn from these lectures at the Odéon ; they are merely pious family gatherings for dusting dramatic relics, valueless to all except those who have inherited them. So that young authors are left to themselves in the midst of a chaotic collection of worn-out models and rough sketches, solicited on every side by the most diverse and contradictory tendencies, and exhausting themselves in attempts to conciliate the incompatible, or endeavouring to be themselves and yet unable to find those selves when they look for them.

V.

THE NEW COMEDY.

WE have touched on Jules Lemaître, the critic,
but we must dwell at much greater length upon
Jules Lemaître, the dramatic author. The two
men are not, after all, so very different; they
only appear so at the first glance, because the
qualities of the one have become the defects of
the other, and *vice versâ*. But upon reflection
the dualism vanishes, and there remains only
Jules Lemaître, the moralist. For I must
reiterate the truth, which seems to have astonished some of my readers; we are a nation
of psychologists and moral philosophers. This
very characteristic, indeed, makes us from time
to time fall a stage behind other nations, for
whilst we are studying our own minds, they
are taking action and making progress; even

their literature is a literature of discovery and advance.

Both his age and his early education, which dates back to the last years of the Empire, make Jules Lemaître belong to the past. He assumed the *toga virilis* when Dumas and Augier were Consuls. From them he received those first theatrical impressions which determine a youth's vocation and give a permanent turn to his literary bent. Both as student at the Ecole Normale and as professor, he belonged to a society, and a select society. For ten years he wrote in a paper where tradition is all powerful, and recently he has been admitted to the Academy, the most reactionary and most essentially aristocratic body in France. His lines are cast, therefore, in a society of the most dominant and absorbing character, in spite of the easy liberalism of its principles and its ingratiating cordiality. In such surroundings the most independent mind can hardly help being moulded into a certain shape. On the other hand, M. Jules Lemaître has seen everything, read everything, and understood everything. Schopenhauer, Tolstoi, Ibsen, have passed before the prism of his mind, casting images which dwindle and vanish and break into a thousand colours. From his stall as a critic he has seen the death of one school and the birth of another. He has borne witness to the faults of the " well-constructed play," with its over-elaborated intrigues and its abuse of wit. He has assisted at the bankruptcy of the naturalist school and taken note of its causes. He has said, "This is good, that is less good. This may be taken, that is worth nothing, the other might be taken with a makeweight." And in this wise he has arrived at eclecticism.

All his plays hitherto have been experiments. He gave us political and social satire in *Le Député Leveau*, psychology in *Le Mariage Blanc*, more psychology, but pitched in quite another key, in *Le Pardon*, something very like a *comédie-rosse* in *L'Age difficile*, a little academic jesting in *La Bonne Hélène*, and lastly in *Les Rois*, a modern tragedy containing all the qualities of a historical play except its history, and even that might be there perhaps if one made diligent search till one found it. His first piece, *Révoltée*, stands alone as being of every style and every sort; but that has nothing to do with eclecticism. It is just a "first play," sketched out, thrown aside, taken up again and finished, then despised, but picked up and re-modelled, carried about in one's portfolio for long enough after being carried still longer in one's head. Crowded into it haphazard are all the thoughts, feelings, and experiences, between the twentieth and thirtieth year, reminiscences (literary and personal), tears, theories, hates, dreams, loves, disillusionment, fury, all that makes up youth!

Révoltée contains one character and one situation. A woman in society has in her youth committed a fault, which she has succeeded in concealing. From afar she has watched over the child born of that fault, but without reveal-ing herself, letting the child suppose her a friend of its mother's. The girl is grown up and married to a professor with gifts and a future. But Hélène, either because of her secret birth or because of her husband's position, has all the thirst for luxury and for emotions, which her modest means can never satisfy. It is quite true that, owing to the peculiar constitution of Parisian society, the wife of a professor gets an insight into high life without being able to play a part in it. She belongs to the aristocracy of intelligence, which in many ways and in many places rubs elbows with the aristocracies of birth and money. She can cherish the illusion that she is of the elect up to the moment when the countess, or the banker's wife, gets into the carriage and drives off, bespattering passers-by like herself, as she trudges back to her fifth-floor apartment. If she is to go to a ball, even in a dyed dress and a few shabby trinkets, her husband must slave away with his pupils from morning till night. It is all very well to go on telling her that he is a man of solid worth; you can't love a slave, and a slave has no time to make love. Is that all? No, the worst vexations and the bitterest stings are just those with no definite name and no assignable cause, diseases whose effects one can see clearly enough without being able to state the cause, or the seat of the evil, or its remedy. Hélène is in revolt—revolt against everything—against life, against society, against religion, against the husband who loves her too much, yet does not love her enough, against the mother who gave her all these cravings and affinities, with nothing that can answer to them. When this mother at last reveals herself and stretches out her arms, the daughter, instead of falling into them, stands feeling her pulse and questioning herself, and then, finding that she feels nothing, refuses the scene of effusion expected of her. This is hard enough for poor Madame de Voves, who thought that she had expiated her fault; but it is harder still to face the absolute and contemptuous condemnation that falls from the lips of her son. When she has forced herself to a half-confession in the hope of interesting him in Hélène, and is pleading the cause of the guilty mother, she only encounters the pitiless arguments of a virtue that will make no sort of allowance, the virtue of a moralist of twenty-five years old. She has to pursue her sad avowal to the bitter end. In the indifference of her daughter and the contempt of her son she finds her own punishment.

It is impossible to listen to Jules Lemaître's Hélène without being forcibly reminded of Augier's Gabrielle. The same nameless unrest, the same aversion for any man who works, no matter whether it be at science or at law. Probably Hélène looked upon the volume of Euclid lying on the drawing-room table much as Gabrielle looked upon "that fat ugly book," the *Code*. I don't blame M. Jules Lemaître for returning, in 1890, to the psychology of the woman who is bored, or for individualising and dating her by means of new and special features. The thing was done long before Augier did it, and will be done again long after M. Jules Lemaître. But it is a real misfortune that he could find no other conclusion than his predecessor's. To regain his wife's love, the Professor—like the Lawyer—has to abandon, nay, even to belie his own character; for a few short hours the poor little bourgeois must draw the sword and play the gallant as principal in a duel, must flaunt himself, in fact, in heroic guise. By to-morrow the hero will have vanished, and the Professor gone back to professing "If A B C be a triangle "; and where will Hélène's heart be then ?

Le Député Leveau aimed at being a complete study of actual political conditions, or, at any rate, of what they were six years ago, for the situation changes quickly. The artist had covered his whole canvas. Instead of one deputy we had three: the Radical, the man of the *nouvelles couches ;* the Liberal of the Left Centre; and the Member of the Right, the man of monarchical and aristocratic traditions. The first represented the primitive sap, the strength which resides in the people, the second the intelligence that belongs to the *bourgeoisie.* And what did the third represent ? Honour, the spirit of chivalry ? *Mon Dieu !* no. He represented nothing but *chic,* truly a mighty power ! Socialism was not so much as suggested, an omission which undoubtedly contributed to make the piece soon seem antiquated. It corresponds very imperfectly to the actual situation, to the present relation of parties and grouping of social forces. Besides, I think, I am hardly mistaken in supposing that the deputy, as material for the drama or the novel, is played out. These people have ceased to be interesting. France is weary of them.

Moreover, one must admit that the play had quite enough faults of its own, without having to struggle against extraneous disadvantages. Only one of the three deputies is alive, both the others are mere lay figures. The gentleman of the Left Centre has a pretty gift of talking, but he does nothing. From the first scene to the last he has only one attitude and one phrase. The gentleman of the Right is an exasperating nonentity; he has only one scene, and he makes nothing out of it. His wife is the real deputy; she might have been a living being, but she only succeeds in being the stage *grande dame*, just a part for Madame Hading, all gowns and smiles. M. Jules Lemaître might, without much difficulty, have found some better models, and some rather more interesting and complex types amongst the older French society.

Leveau is only partially successful. Is it vanity, or is it passion, which throws him at the feet of that insipid Marquise? Or is it both?

Is he not abusing the right of the heart to be "a simpleton," to quote a celebrated lover? He is a little childish and absurd when he talks about love, but he is himself again when he gets into a passion, and he is really superb in the fourth act, when he turns upon his allies of yesterday and denounces the party that has proved so fatal to him. Madame Leveau is what she needs must be, a querulous stranger from the provinces, utterly devoid of tact or charm. She confides in the first comer, and her whining complaints are perfectly endless. She gets on our nerves, and pretty nearly disgusts us outright, when she laments out loud, and in her daughter's presence, the rupture of conjugal intimacy. But what a good, honest soul she is after all, and how gallantly she defends her name, and her home, and the rights of her child! How that tongue-tied, ignorant woman imposes silence upon the tribune, whose very profession is eloquence! The *petite bourgeoisie* of France, with its honourable absurdities and its unlovely virtues, has seldom been better depicted on the stage, but perhaps the very truth and moderation of the portrait account for its apparent dulness and indefiniteness, and the soporific effect which it creates on the spectators. Madame Leveau is a character for a novel.

The fact is that at heart M. Lemaître is bored with the study of the primitive desires of an uncultivated *parvenu*. In *Le Mariage Blanc*, which he first carried to the Rue Richelieu, he found a subject far better suited to his delicate talent. Down in a quiet corner of that Mediterranean coast, which combines the poetry of health restored with the attractions of a life of pleasure, where some come to live faster and others to die more gently, a mother is living with her two daughters, one beautiful and full of health, the other a fascinating little creature on the verge of the grave, whose love of life and power of loving seem only quickened by the approach of death. Everyone crowds round Simone, and is eager to gratify her lightest whim. The three women have planned their whole way of living in the hope of saving or prolonging that cherished life. As for Marthe, she is well; what more can she ask? She is not interesting. What matters it if her five-and-twenty years and her wonderful beauty (it was Mdlle. Marsy who played the part, the inevitable Mdlle. Marsy!) waste away in a solitude, where they can never attract the attention of a husband?

However, there is one man in this household whose presence is a little agitating to the two girls. He is a world-weary melancholy creature who has loved much and philosophised more. His sensual nature has been appeased and fined away but not extinguished, and it has left room enough in his soul for pity to slip in. For a man of his age and temper there is but one problem left to solve, one rare sensation which can still attract him. Of the two girls whom chance has thrown in his way he sees only one, the one whom death is claiming, and it occurs to him to give the poor doomed child the illusion of one day's bliss. He will marry Simone. The way in which he makes his declaration to the young girl, persuades the mother, and silences the doctor's scruples, is indicated with that supreme cleverness which foresees every objection and lifts every rock out of the path.

Simone seems to receive new life. She has forgotten that she had just been speaking of marrying her sister to M. de Tièvre, and that she had almost entrapped Marthe into an avowal. Perhaps, then, she is not thought beyond hope since she is to be married? The wish to live returns with the joy of loving.

They are married. But how is M. de Tièvre going to play his part of husband-nurse? Will he keep up the illusion and complete the good deed? Indeed, is it a good deed? If it could be said that to the pure all things are pure, might one not say with even greater show of reason that to those who have lived mainly by the senses, all things are sensual, even pity and devotion. We needs must end by grasping this truth, even if we have not already felt it; there is something besides abnegation, charity, sacrifice, in this intimacy between a man, who knows too much of life, and a child, who knows it not at all, who believes herself a wife because she is married, and reveals all her maiden heart to her husband. For all M. Lemaître's discretion, he might have shown a little more, and I can assure him that the Théâtre Français is doing him a service, when it omits certain words and phrases, whose meaning is a little too clear. Even from the point of view of art pure and simple, some ideas gain by being only suggested.

This strange intimacy which won that *blasé* heart by its very strangeness, becomes sensibly warmer, as the young wife seems to take firmer hold upon existence. False situations are the sweetest of all, and this singular husband and wife would have gone on enjoying their oddly constituted happiness, made of reticences and misapprehensions, if the cry of real living passion, the cry of a soul in pain, had not broken the charm. Who uttered the cry? Who but Marthe, whom all have forgotten, and who could not take back her love, nor give up the hope of being loved. M. de Tièvre falters for a moment before the love that he has awakened in the heart of this beautiful girl, Simone sees the weakness, and it kills her.

Le Pardon is a very fine work, and some admirers of M. Lemaître prefer it to all his others. Certainly he never displayed to better advantage his real mastery of the art of expressing the fine shades and gradations of human emotion. Nor has he ever better vindicated his title to stand beside Dumas as a moralist. But it must be admitted that M. Lemaître's morality would scarcely serve as a code of rules for ordinary conduct. Morality ought to be something as solid and as capable of resistance as the umbrella of a countryman going to market, but M. Lemaître's morality is at best only the elegant *en tout cas* of a pretty woman on her way to the Grand Prix. What will become of this supple, flexible, subtle, almost voluptuous view of life, when confronted with the hail of human passion and the soft, persistent, and penetrating rain of human sophistry? Take the case of Georges and Suzanne. Apparently to repent is easy enough, but to pardon almost impossible, unless one has oneself been guilty of the same fault. Then, indeed, in absolving the other sinner one absolves oneself, and it is so easy to be indulgent in one's own case. The idea is paradoxical, but not quite new. Dumas dealt with it in *Francillon*. But here it is the woman who has sinned first. She is allowed to return to wedded life, only to be tortured by stinging questions, humiliated by cruel memories and still more cruel comparisons, and insulted by constantly recurring doubts. So it goes on until the day, when a certain lady who has played the dangerous part of counsellor, accepts the still more dangerous part of consoler. Are the husband and wife at daggers drawn again? On the contrary, they are reconciled for good and all. The husband's adultery annuls the wife's; the two faults are both cancelled at once, like two equal quantities on two sides of an equation.

There, only much more delicately handled, you have the inevitable dénouement of the Théâtre Libre : " I am worth nothing, and you are not worth very much, let us kiss and be friends ! " M. Lemaître was still more "théâtre-libre" in *L'Age difficile;* but at the eleventh hour he repented, like the penitent thief, and exactly at a quarter to twelve we found ourselves floating in pure optimism and all the virtues. What with her husband, an adventurer, and her father, an old knight of the pavement, whose moral sense has entirely evaporated in thirty years of *fête*, Yoyo is a highly amusing little rascal, but as repulsive as the heroines of M. Jean Jullien and Paul Alexis. M. Jules Lemaître is amazingly witty. If he had been born five-and-twenty years sooner he would have been called Edmond About, fifty years sooner Prosper Mérimée. Consequently there must be in him a strain of heroism, else he would not write plays in which wit can have no place, unless he is inspired by the very legitimate, if coquettish, desire to prove his possession of other and still more precious gifts. Anyhow, with the exception of a few stray sayings in the first act of *Révoltée* and the first act of *Le Député Leveau*, M. Lemaître's spectators had been deprived of that original vein of wit which gave such delight to his readers. But throughout *L'Age difficile* there is a ceaseless flow of wit without in any way detracting from his delicate moral perception. The explanation between the faithless Pierre and his wife, Jeanne, at the beginning of the second act is perfectly delightful, and would be a masterpiece of truth and comedy if its admirable beginning did not tail off into pedantic and somewhat wearisome argument. But to explain the title of the play, I must say one word about the principal character —the character that makes the play. Which is the difficult age? The sixtieth year. Doubtless this age is not difficult to the man who understands how to grow old, and who has been careful to lay up a store of affection for the time of life which cannot hope to gather in fresh harvests. But it is a difficult age for the old bachelor, who consoles himself with left-handed paternity, and is forced to intrude upon other people's happiness if he is to win any for himself. When he sees that he is *de trop*, he rushes headlong into another danger; Yoyo. These two syllables suggest such a mingled aroma of childishness and corruption that I need not go on. What can save him from Yoyo? The friendship of a pure and innocent woman, rising out of the dead ashes of the past, and ready to resume a dream rudely broken off thirty years ago. Placed between the saint and the good-for-nothing, he chooses the saint. But, unfortunately, she is infinitely less real and life-like than the other, and one fancies that Yoyo will live longer in the memories of spectators of all ages. This dénouement is all very good and proper, but I fear that it is not much better than that of *Le Pardon.*

I am nowise discouraged by the fact that *Les Rois* met with a sufficiently cold reception from the public. Probably it is M. Lemaître's best play, and except, perhaps, *Le Mariage Blanc,* the play most within his compass. It begins like one of Dumas' pieces. Some by-standers, who never reappear, put us *au courant* with the situation and the characters. The second act has a new *exposition,* meant to introduce us to Prince Otto, after all rather a minor character, and Acts III. and IV. contain the action of the play, which took so much setting in motion. For the ordinary spectator the piece is practically at an end with the death of the hero, and, but for the presence of Sarah Bernhardt, the fifth act would have received scant attention. Yet, both in thought and expression, this fifth act contains gems of the very finest water. Save for the character of Prince Otto, who is obviously borrowed from contemporary history and treated in naturalistic fashion, the play is a tragedy. All the personages, from the king down to the old huntsman, belong to the heroic world, and utter sentiments a little more magnificent than natural. In reading *Les Rois* I felt something of that deep and noble emotion which was awakened in me many years ago by the words of that sublime dreamer, the Marquis of Posa, in Schiller's *Don Carlos.* Doubtless the day will come when the works which stirred our hearts and moved our inmost being will seem cold and affected to future generations, when *Les Rois* will be listened to with the pious respect that we pay to Polyeucte and Athalie. We are in perfect agreement as to the beauty of their form; we fully expect noble thoughts, fine phrases and outbursts of passion, and never trouble ourselves as to whether or not they are really "dramatic" in the narrow sense in which that formula was used from 1840 to 1890. By that time the faults in the construction of *Les Rois* will trouble no one, and the conclusion, which now seems confused, will be as clear as day, when historic evolution has done its work. Then we shall know that the struggle between monarchy and democracy is indeed a struggle without an end, that kings no longer possess the power to rule, nor the right to devote their lives to their subjects, nay, not even the right to abandon those rights. They have but one last sad duty, to await the end, crowned and sceptred, maintaining intact that inheritance of the past, which is doomed to pass away with them.

We assisted at M. Brieux' brilliant début amidst the writers for the Théâtre Libre, with *Blanchette* and *Ménages d'Artistes*. He is accused by some of having greatly changed, whilst others see in this change matter for congratulation. Personally, I do not think the transformation as complete as people suppose. If M. Antoine had looked closer, he would have discerned both in *Blanchette* and in *Ménages d'Artistes* the germ of the problem play, the very name of which was enough to give him a fit. M. Brieux has since taken firmer ground as a critic and a satirist, a very different attitude from that of the anatomical impassive artist demanded by the naturalist school. He has had the audacity to draw conclusions. And why not? If it is an interesting problem, why not an interesting play? Must we, as an excellent critic said recently, forbear to present any idea on the stage until it has penetrated into people's souls and become a sentiment, or even until this sentiment has become a passion? Is it not enough that the sentiment should be a passion to the writer of the play, as the equality of the sexes was to Dumas fils? Can a drama turn on nothing but the passions themselves? Cannot its subject be the birth of those sentiments, which originate in ideas, in the conflict of interests, or the laws of society? To my mind such a drama is both possible and much to be desired.

But the writer of such a play, a play which instead of dealing with the private caprices of So-and-so, attacks professions, classes, institutions, the principles of conduct that govern society, needs to be something more than an ingenious satirist endowed with observation and wit. He must have studied and reflected much, he must be a man of robust convictions and perfectly sure of himself. He must neither miss his aim, nor strike at random, nor attack everything at once, nor involve in one common satire the guilty, the ignorant, the blundering, and those whose only crime is to have failed. M. Brieux has aimed his shafts successively at popular education (*Blanchette*), at art (*Ménages d'Artistes*), at science (*L'Evasion*), at universal suffrage (*L'Engrenage*), and at charity (*Les Bienfaiteurs*). So much the worse for him, if we refuse to believe him, and so much the worse for us, if we laugh with him, for all these things are really good, and we need to preserve them. Oh! I understand; M. Brieux is not jeering at them, he is only criticising those who abuse them and carry them to excess, who travesty them and apply them to false and foolish uses. No doubt, but the drama demands clear issues, and a frank adoption of a side. The "who knows?" the "perhaps," the "yes or no," so appropriate to a fanciful discourse on philosophy, are of no account on the stage. M. Brieux runs a risk of being misunderstood, and, as a rule, when one is misunderstood, one has failed altogether to understand oneself. That has been his fate in at least one instance, *Les Bienfaiteurs.* This play contains some excellent comic episodes, which abundantly prove the writer's talent, especially when it is a question of presenting popular types. But taken as a whole it is disconcerting and almost irritating. At the outset we have much pleasure in making the acquaintance of the engineer Landrecy and his wife. He has invented a beautiful scientific apparatus, and he has certain ideas about the relations between capital and labour, which seem honest and sound. His wife is full of pity for every sort of suffering. Both wish to do good, and are prepared to try and do it. But they lack one thing, a little money. Lo and behold it descends upon them. A brother of Madame Landrecy's, whose family had forgotten him, and who seemed to have forgotten them, turns up with his hands full of millions. He will lend his aid to the double experiment. Landrecy can set his invention going in his works, and can invite his workpeople to share its profits. Madame Landrecy can realise her schemes for the relief of the sick and poor, and the reformation and elevation of the fallen. But things do not turn out as they had hoped, and the public, which had bestowed such hearty approval upon their beautiful dreams, shares their disappointment, and is saddened and almost humiliated by their failure. It is easy enough to see that the mistaken, misguided, and misdirected benevolence of Madame Landrecy and her friends, often favour sham repentance to the detriment of honest industry, that electoral ambition, and the rivalry of schools, parties, and society mingle with charity and mar it, that it gives the flirt her opportunity, that it calls into existence an ugly class of hypocrites, the officials, the red-tapists of charity. We see these "benefactors" much abashed by the suicide which they could not hinder, crowding officiously round the corpse and attempting sophistical exculpations. Certainly these are some of the sins of charity. Admit for the moment a palpable absurdity, namely, that these sins counterbalance and neutralise all the good that is done in the world; still there is Landrecy. His invention was genuine, and his economic theory —that the workmen should share in the profits —was sound and reasonable. What evil had he done? None, but that he believed in the goodness and intelligence of the people, and that he had been a little stiff and petulant with his obstinate workmen, when he found out his mistake. Then why involve him in his wife's disgrace and oblige the young man to listen to a lecture, which he has not deserved? Simply because M. Brieux is not content with attacking one problem, which is too much for him, but must needs attack two, the extinction of pauperism and the organization of labour, nothing less than that! It is too much for one single evening, it would even be too much for one single life. What are we told about charity? That we ought to practise it, but that it is very difficult indeed to practise it rightly; that charity does not consist in giving alms; that we must treat those whom we benefit as human beings, and "convey our benefit in friendly words," &c. But Landrecy and his wife, and all of us knew that after the first Act, and even perhaps before a child of the male sex named Eugènc Brieux had been inscribed on the civil registers. I can see clearly the moral that egoism will deduce from this play, a nice, easy moral—complete abstention. And it will be a pity, for goodness is worth much even when mis- placed, and devotion, even when unenlightened ; it is better, to quote M. Faguet's witty phrase, to do good ill than to do ill well.

If the position maintained in *Les Bienfaiteurs* is not clear enough, that of *L'Evasion* is much too clear. It is more than a satire—it is a frantic attack upon science. Pseudo science ? No, real science, the science which we are accustomed to respect, and ought to respect. In the first place, it is a little unfair to personify science in a doctor. Forced as he is by his profession to make it an article of commerce, he is tempted to certain compromises which diminish and degrade it. He may be a great savant and at the same time a great charlatan, and let us admit at once that

Dr. Bertry is both. But just as Catholics count the Mass valid although the priest is unworthy, science remains science in spite of the unworthiness of her representative.

There are many points on which M. Brieux has failed to understand his great adversary. He has made war upon her without completing his equipment. If he had made a careful study of the writings of Francis Galton, whose name he quotes twice, he would recognise the fact of regression, and he would know that selection corrects heredity instead of intensifying it, because it constantly tends to approximate to the normal type. Nevertheless, speaking generally, Dr. Bertry's theory of the transmission of instincts is true, and it is a theory which conflicts with the idea of freewill, upon which our society is based, and which is indispensable to our creeds and codes. It might indeed harmonize with the Calvinist and Jansenist doctrine of grace, or even be confused with it, but, I ought to add, that no view could be more antagonistic to the tendencies which prevail in France. M. Brieux relied on this disposition on the part of his audience for his success, and he was within his rights as a dramatic author. But I begin to rub my eyes when I see the Academy solemnly crowning M. Brieux' play. What did it mean to reward? The play or the problem? Certainly the play is not good, but the problem is detestable. In any case, its approval of M. Brieux' work put it in the awkward position of appearing to challenge its sister Academy of Sciences. Let the two ancient dames decide as best they can the standing quarrel between Fatalism and Liberty.

Literature has no part in M. Brieux' success. The Greeks and Romans can claim no share in the formation of his very modern mind. He clothes his thought in the first words that occur to him, the language of everyday talk or of journalism. He is no literary artist, and if he tried to be, he would probably only succeed in attaining the sort of eloquence which made M. Ohnet's reputation. After all, as Labiche proved, one can write excellent plays without a word of literature. M. Brieux' wit is robust and gay. Even when gloom and cruelty were in fashion he could never quite succeed. This was a great defect in Antoine's eyes, but, after all, it is a quality in ordinary theatres. Of course, he has been guilty of a few blunders. Now and again a scene opening with a simple and lifelike situation, and up to a certain point skilfully worked out, comes to an abrupt end, or loses itself in dissertations and declamations, or turns round, without rhyme or reason, and plunges into frantic melodrama. But every day will see him more master of his trade, and already he has few equals in putting a story on the stage. I was tempted to parody old Sylla's epigram, and to say that I see several Sardous in this young man. But then I went to see *Les Trois Filles de M. Dupont.* It is a leap backwards, a return to the savage and pessimist traditions of the Théâtre Libre— to the play which is no play, only a procession of characters; to the dénouement which is no dénouement, but an angry confession of impotence. There is no movement in the drama, it never advances a single step. Of M. Dupont's three daughters the saint will remain a saint without faith, the courtesan will remain a courtesan without love, the daughter unhappily married will remain unhappily married, and go on cursing her husband, and proposing to deceive him. There is no end to their trials, no cure for their ills. It is a universal and absolute condemnation of the existing social order.

Strange to say, at the very moment when M. Brieux was giving us this ominous and despairing fourth act of *Les Trois Filles de M. Dupont*, he had just tacked on an optimist ending to *Blanchette*, which seems much to the taste of the public. Which side of M. Brieux will win : the quick, energetic personality, the combative nature that can only find solace and serenity in the joy of fighting; or the gloomy, disintegrating melancholy of the decadent group, who try to monopolise him? I incline to the first hypo- thesis. Whatever school may reign, and from whatever quarter the wind may blow, every mind follows its own bent and works with its own gifts. These things are governed by the same law that rules the changes of fashion. Though skirts be long, have no fear for the woman with a pretty foot; nor if fringes come down to the nose, for her with a pretty forehead. Both will find some way of displaying their natural advantages, however much the fashion of the moment may be against them.

Doubtless this is why M. Henri Lavedan's wit has captivated a generation which is for ever depreciating that quality and pretending to get on very well without it. If I am not mistaken, Henri Lavedan's maiden effort consisted of some little society dialogues which appeared in *La Vie Parisienne*, work of a kind, charming in itself but not of yesterday, nor even of yesteryear, for are not Theocritus' *Syracusan Women* and Lucian's *Dialogues of Courtesans* delightful examples? Without going so far back, one may mention the success achieved thirty years ago by Henri Meilhac's sketches. But there is a marked difference in one respect between M. Lavedan and his predecessor. Meilhac was the faithful, ingenious, ironical, and much-amused delineator of the gay world of Paris, which he loved, and out of which he could not live. With Henri Lavedan it is more often guesswork than observation. He never plays with his model, either before or after the sitting, as some artists do; indeed, has he any models? Is he not one of those writers who can construct a whole scene or a character out of a chance phrase overheard in passing? In short, he has more invention, more humour, and more of the unexpected about him, he is more human and more profound than his predecessor, and underlying the mockery, one can feel in him more than in any other writer of his time, emotion, goodness, tenderness, a great respect for all that is pure, a great pity for all that is weak. I think that, in spite of the excessive freedom of his portraiture, he would find friends in England. But how could one translate that inimitable style, so delicate and artistic in its disorder and disarray, with its fantastic grammar and amazing slang, its abbreviations, its brusquerie, its almost imperceptible suggestions breaking off into phrases, which strike one dumb. Some smart fellow will doubtless presume to try. Even *Tartarin* has been translated!

M. Lavedan has not been so misguided as to attempt to transfer any of those Tanagra-like figures, half doll, half statuette, from the idyls of the decadence, to which they belong, to the stage where they would be almost invisible. In his plays, proportion, relief, attitudes, everything is regulated according to the old laws of theatrical optics. His style also becomes broader and more emphatic. But there is the same psychology, the same boldness in attack, and even greater vividness. *Le Prince d'Aurec* had a brilliant success, all the more brilliant because it gave rise to burning controversies. The older aristocracy complained bitterly of the libel, all the more because it came from the son of one of their most energetic defenders. As a matter of fact, M. Henri Lavedan is the son of M. Léon Lavedan, whose proud, unbending character and high-minded genius command universal respect. But did the father's forty years' record of honourable devotion and political fidelity bind the son to a cause, which has since passed out of the region of facts to that of memories? The question is easy enough to answer, but to my mind it ought not even to have been asked. I see in *Le Prince d'Aurec* a friendly warning; not a hostile gibe. What charge would an enemy bring against the French *noblesse?* That it clings convulsively to its traditions. But M. Lavedan's charge is just the opposite, that it forgets them.

The Prince d'Aurec is the modern gentleman whose creed can be summed up in two words, to be chic and to go the pace. Half-a-century ago a man so placed and with similar tastes married M. Poirier's daughter. That is what the prince's father, the Duc de Talais did. He took to wife Mdlle. Piédoux, who had the glory of being duchess at the price of a few millions and an infinite deal of domestic humiliation. In her old age and widowhood, and with a son who promises to be worse than his father, she has betaken herself to aristocratic snobbishness and the veneration of parchments. And it is amusing to hear a Piédoux talking with enthusiastic and devoted respect of traditions and ancestors, whilst a d'Aurec makes merciless fun of everything of the kind. We laughed at the good lady through two acts, all unconscious that we should have to admire her at the dénouement.

The Prince has an immense fund of wit

because M. Lavedan has endowed him with his own. One cannot help joining in his gibes at the class and party to which he belongs, the last remnants of the Gothic age, the few surviving adherents of the throne and altar. But he is not content with gibes; he raises money on his title deeds and heirlooms. A hundred years ago on that famous night of the 4th August, in which the d'Aurecs must have borne their share, the French *noblesse* offered up their privileges on the altar of their country; he on the contrary prefers to carry them to the pawn-broker. He sells the sword of the Constable d'Aurec as if it were an ordinary piece of bric-à-brac; he sells his friendship to a certain Jewish Baron, who by advancing him considerable sums has gradually become his master, and what is more serious, the master of the princess, for precisely similar reasons, since she also is in his debt.

Why a Jew? I do not think that M. Lavedan intended for one moment to take part in the odious and preposterous crusade that has been waged these ten years back against the Israelitish

element in Parisian society. De Horn represents
the power of money. Now money has neither
creed nor country, but it is an abstract power
which needs to be reinforced by a living passion,
and that passion needs to be given a human
countenance. The Jew immediately occurs to
the imagination, the Jew with his mysterious
psychology, his unchangeable type subsisting
through the ages, his deep undying ancestral
hatreds, which make him in this dawn of the
twentieth century the avenger of the tortures of
the twelfth and thirteenth. The Jew ever since
the days of Marlowe and Shakespeare has
haunted the artistic imagination. Shylock is an
obsession second only to Hamlet. To me Baron
de Horn seems merely a Shylock in lavender
kid gloves, concealing his rage under the cool
exterior of a gentleman, but a figure to strike
terror in the scene where he too comes to claim
the pound of human flesh, that has been offered
him as a pledge. The princess is his destined
prey, and her beauty is to pay his debt. There
is the wild beast's thirst, the slave's hope of
vengeance, but with it all a deeply-laid scheme

of policy. A d'Aurec the mistress of a de Horn, the conjunction is symbolical of the prostitution of one aristocracy to another; it will fix both for us and for those who come after us a really critical and decisive moment in the history of manners. The victims, alive to their danger, struggle like wild things caught in a trap; it is a splendid and horrible spectacle, but it is all in vain. They could never escape if the old duchess, who, Piédoux though she be, is the only member of the family with the soul of a d'Aurec, had not stripped herself so as to purchase the right to rout the intruder. But it is only a stage dénouement after all. De Horn keeps the Constable's sword, that sword which is symbolical of warlike courage and devotion to the common weal, the old ideal of chivalry, the source of the greatness and strength of the ancient *noblesse.* All is lost, even honour.

M. Lavedan has combated the objections that have been made in an odd little act, which is scarcely more than a polemical article in dialogue, and which he has called, following Molière, *la Critique du Prince d'Aurec.* The sole charge to which he might perhaps plead guilty, is that of not having indicated where, in his opinion, lies the only hope for the restoration of the ancient aristocracy. Instead of allying itself with the fungous growths of the Bourse, and begging for a share in the great financial swindles of the day, let it gain new strength from work, and let it seek less for the reward that work brings, than for the virtues which it fosters. That is the idea represented by M. Lavedan in *Les Deux Noblesses.* The action of the second play is placed forty years later than that of the first. For an almost new-born child must be given time to grow to manhood, and to have, in his turn, a grown-up son. Consequently *Le Prince d'Aurec*, which seemed to us to correspond so closely to the social symptoms of 1890 that it might well have been called *Le Fils du Gendre de M. Poirier*, must be relegated to a remote past, where it will very likely seem an anachronism. We are the more disconcerted because the play that is assigned to our own days seems much older, both in idea and in its selection of characters. The Marquis de

Touringe is another Marquis de la Seiglière; we have gone back to the days when a nobleman of ancient family found it a hard task, and a sacrifice of caste, to marry a roturier's daughter. We might get over that first shock, if the fundamental idea of the play afforded firm standing ground. But it does no such thing. The son of that Prince d'Aurec, who scandalised us and amused us so greatly, has been brought up in America, and has voluntarily abjured both his name and title. He is M. Roche " the French petroleum king," and he is so well satisfied with the change, and so set on remaining one of the people, that he conceals the secret of his birth from his own son, and this when a revelation would remove every obstacle to a marriage which the young man ardently desires. An enemy accepts the task of making the disclosure, but with a result that contradicts all his hopes. For the workmen, who were just about to strike, change their minds at once. They are gratified by their master's rank, and shout at the top of their voices, "Vive le Prince d'Aurec!" Those workmen are not far wrong, and seem to enter into M. Lavedan's idea of the rehabilitation of the old *noblesse* by work, much more than the hero of the play or the daughter of the Marquis, who, when she enters her new family circle, declares that she wishes to bear the plebeian name of Madame Henri Roche. But that is no rehabilitation, it is an abdication. The chain of tradition is broken, shattered for ever. The Roches may win a place by their merits in the first rank of the new society, but the d'Aurecs are no more. There will always be an aristocracy, that is to say a ruling class, but there will be no more *noblesse*, that is to say an exclusive or semi-exclusive caste, handing on from generation to generation a certain ideal of honour and devotion, a body of unchangeable rights and duties. M. Lavedan's play—if plays have any influence on social evolution—could only teach the old aristocracy one lesson, how to die nobly. But they could not if they would. A class cannot take refuge in suicide; it is not given to it, as to an individual, to die at a stroke. Neither the night of the 4th of August, nor the law of 1848, which abolished titles, put an end to the existence of the *noblesse.* It cannot escape the ignominy of gradual atrophy and progressive degradation. Democratic snobbishness even now offers it a last chance. It will live from hand to mouth as it did during the days of the emigration, when one of its members made a livelihood out of his superior skill in mixing salads. It will give lessons in deportment to banker barons and political *parvenus.* It will polish them up, and they will keep it from starvation. So much for its future.

Les Deux Noblesses had another defect over and above the weakness of its plot; only at rare intervals was there any suggestion of the author's charming and fantastic humour. It was the fault of the subject. But we get M. Lavedan back again in *Viveurs,* one of the great successes of the theatrical season of 1895-6. As we passed from the fitting-rooms of a great *couturier* to the big supper-room of a restaurant, we were introduced to the gay world, not the professionals—they are bored and gloomy enough —but the mad crowd of pleasure-seekers, those who work by day and live by night, a strange crowd, where the feminine element is represented by young girls partly compromised, and married women who have no more reputation to lose. Half frightened, half amused, we looked on at the giddy farandole led by Réjane with inimitable *brio*. In the second act she jumped over a table to get back to her lover. All through the piece she jumped over all our old ideas of decorum and *bourgeois* morals. But at the end she owned herself conquered, she confessed herself guilty, and the skill of the actress, aided by that of the author, made this highly artificial conversion both touching and convincing. For all that it was a mere trick, and I think that M. Lavedan is called to higher things. Who knows whether it will not rest with him to put honest folk on the stage again ? *

* *Catherine,* which was played so successfully at the Théâtre Français in February last, has fully justified these anticipations. At the same moment *Le Nouveau Jeu,* which has been running over a hundred consecutive nights at the Variétés, showed that Lavedan was a greater master than ever in the art of lifelike portraiture, and had lost none of his knowledge of the ways and humours of the gay world.

VI.

THE NEW COMEDY—*(continued)*.

THE most striking and original amongst the younger men who have come to light during the last five or six years, the two who sound a really new note in dramatic literature, are Paul Hervieu and Maurice Donnay, and I do not think that any critic with a love of antithesis has ever lighted on a contrast more strongly marked. Hervieu and Donnay are as absolutely opposed as will and temperament; laborious effort and improvisation; shadow and light; winter and summer; north and south; hatred and love of life. Both look on at the same world, but the one with the eyes of a Stoic, the other of an Epicurean. In that eternal question of marriage, adultery, divorce, from which neither our stage nor our society can escape; in that duel between the sexes which, in our days, has become so strongly accentuated, Hervieu is the declared defender of the rights of the woman, Donnay the crafty advocate of the failings and passions of the man. To put the matter in a nutshell, I think that the law has seldom been better attacked than by the first, or love better defended than by the second.

A few years ago I met M. Paul Hervieu in a newspaper office. I remember a pale, interesting, finely-cut face, suggesting the idea of nervous energy in repose, grave, almost melancholy eyes, no shadow of a smile, no suspicion of a gesture, an even, colourless, indifferent voice, nothing affected or irritating, but an evident determination to keep himself to himself, and not to wear his heart upon his sleeve. This was before M. Hervieu's first success, when his name was scarcely known to anyone except brethren of the trade. An eminent *artiste*, who holds a high place in Parisian society, was, if I am not mistaken, one of the first to understand him, and to introduce him. His novel, *Flirt*, was much read. It was such an attractive title, and the book did more than justify the promise of the

title. I remember that it pleased women of the
world because it was so delicate in form, and said
very audacious things very prettily. Moreover,
it was lighted. up here and there by those touches
of mischief which they like, without ever falling
into that coarser mirth which they detest. This
veiled gaiety disappeared in the succeeding
novels. I confess that I was very much bored
by these, and that I understood very little of
them. M. Hervieu seemed to me to be develop-
ing a dismal preciosity. His efforts to evolve a
style were scarcely happy ; moreover, what is
the use of torturing words, trampling on old
phrases, and disturbing our minds in a hundred
ways, if, after all, the idea that one is trying to
convey remains formless and vague ? What is
the Sphinx without its enigma ? I was just
admitting that M. Hervieu had struck a bad vein
and was in great danger of deserving the praise
of idiots, when his dramatic successes filled me
with surprise and delight. His three plays—one
played at the Vaudeville, two represented at the
Français—lifted him at once to the first rank,
and showed the world that he was master of a

dramatic manner, as clear, as outspoken, as easy to define, as his style in fiction was subtle, tortuous, and disconcerting.

Les Paroles Restent was M. Paul Hervieu's first appearance on the stage. This is the plot: the Marquis de Nohan, a soldier and a man of the world, has met, in the East, Mdlle. Régine de Vesles, the daughter of a diplomatist. Misled by certain appearances, he believed this young girl to be engaged in a guilty intrigue. He told the story under the seal of most intimate confidence to a woman whom he loved, and she circulated it throughout Parisian society. Régine's reputation was gone. She remained in ignorance of the fact, but the man, who was the cause of the evil, both knew it and deplored it. Not only did he break off all relations with the wretched woman who had let out the secret, but he fell deeply in love with his victim. To complete his remorse, he learns that the circumstances which deceived him admit of quite a natural explanation, and that Régine, for all the freedom of her manners, is purity itself. There is only one way of repairing his fault, and giving the lie

to the reports which he has set on foot. It consists in marrying the woman whom he has
calumniated. Therefore he decides to tell her his
love, but at the same time to confess his fault.
These two confessions, the first so easy if only it
had not to be followed by the cruel second, make
up a very touching scene, although it is spoilt in
some parts by the mannerism, the laboured
subtlety of expression, all too frequent in M.
Hervieu's novels. The Marquis de Nohan, who,
as I have just said, has the two confessions to
make, wants Régine de Vesles to decide which
ought to come first, just as in the Chamber
members dispute the Order of the day. "Suppose
that a man is in a situation like this with a girl
whom he loves,"—then simplifying the case and
coming nearer to the truth—"suppose that I am
that man." In his mortal trouble, in his strange
desire to be both understood and not understood,
he stammers out some ridiculous, scarcely intel-
ligible phrases. "Don't you think that a woman's
unhappiness can only come from one single thing
—from a person?" When Régine, half stifled
by emotion, cries out, "My friend, my friend,

you hurt me!"—then corrects herself—"No, that is only a way of speaking because there are no words to express that one feels something better than good," I feel a great desire to burst out laughing, both at the expression which is so awkward, and at the idea which is so ambiguous, so twisted, so artificial. But I remember the curious perversity of the human heart, which never says frankly all that it means; instead of the simple and direct, it prefers the oblique, the complex. That is what made the fortune of Euphuism and *Marivaudage.* Moreover, the situation here is so embarrassed that the style can hardly fail to feel the effects. At length the truth is out, and the scene, as M. Hervieu has written it, ends pretty much as might have been expected. Régine de Vesles does not accept the reparation which is offered her. It is precisely because she loves her calumniator that she suffers retrospectively in her pride and in her love. In the first moment of passion she adopts as her champion an enigmatical personage, whose character and sentiments are never explained to us. There is a provocation given and a duel; de Nohan is dangerously wounded. His danger brings Régine to his side, forgiving all. He will be cured, doubtless, and they will be happy. No, for the world has not said its last word. As the proverb says, " Les paroles restent." The infamous story is repeated once again in public. De Nohan hears it, and the shock costs him his life.

This dénouement belongs to the purest melodrama. M. Hervieu, in *Les Paroles Restent*, has borrowed a few weapons from the inexhaustible arsenal of Scribe and his followers. The duel, the will which serves to exhibit the beautiful sentiments of the hero and heroine—we know all that, and we have made up our minds that we want no more of it. The author has also been reproached for letting so many characters hover about in the background, just as Dumas did, a method hurtful to unity, by which I mean the only true and necessary unity, unity of impression. But M. Hervieu might have replied that these secondary characters are only the Hydra's heads, the fragments of that formidable and mysterious entity, which delights to devour reputations and shirks all responsibility. Don't try and banish these people from the piece, for they play a much more important part in it than the pale figure of de Nohan.

M. Hervieu did better than answer. Three years later, in *Les Tenailles*, he gave us a play exempt from these faults. Not only does it show a considerable advance on the last play, but it seems to improve as it goes on. At the beginning there are a few tortuous, subtle sentences; in the final act all is bitter, concentrated, poignant. Irene Fergan has been married for ten years to a man whom she does not love. Why does she cherish a grudge against him? Just because he has not known how to make himself loved. She is told that she will love him when she is married. "It was not I who was married ten years ago, it was the other woman that I was then." But she does not tell us all. She loves Michel Davernier, the celebrated traveller, who, on his side, cherishes a great heroic passion for her. Will she yield to him like so many other women, who take a lover and preserve the outward appearance of virtue? Will she lie, deceive, smile in the face of the man whom she detests? No, rather a thousand times divorce. She goes straïght to her husband and tells him of her resolution. But Robert Fergan does not see the matter at all in the same light, neither does the law. He explains to her with his calm and cruel irony that you cannot go and say to the judges, "This man and I thought we loved one another. We made a mistake. We desire to be set free." What grievance will she allege? — adultery, ill-usage, serious insult? Nothing of the sort exists, and consequently it cannot be proved. Moreover, there must be a motive. "Well," cries Irene, "we will invent one." That, I think, is what the English law calls "collusion." Our law, less far-sighted and less strict, leaves the door open to these little conspiracies. But in such a case the husband must be the accomplice to the wife. Now Robert Fergan had no intention of getting a divorce. "And if I run away?" "I will have you brought back by the gendarmes." "And if I disgrace your name?" "I will keep you all the same." Thus, according to the French law, which regulates marriage and divorce, the wife is the prisoner of the husband, and must remain such at her jailor's good pleasure. That is the first situation, the first striking moment of the play.

This is the second. Ten years have elapsed. The victim has apparently become resigned, and the husband and wife seem to have lived together on fairly good terms, away from the world, in a lonely country place, where M. Fergan has chosen to shut up his wife. A child has been born, little René, and it is on his account that the struggle begins again. The father has decided to send him to school; the mother means to keep him at home. Every argument has been exhausted on both sides, and it rests with M. Fergan to insist on getting his own way. "He belongs to me, his father." "You are not his father," and she confesses that on one occasion, maddened by her galling chains, she had put aside all generous scruples and had yielded to the man she loved. The child is hers, hers only. But here Fergan remembers the law, which puts the child into his hands. What is he thinking of?—some cowardly vengeance? She cries shame upon him. Can a civilised man make a victim of a child, appease his wounded pride by sacrificing a weak, helpless creature who, for ten years, he has thought to be his own flesh and blood? At that moment little René crosses the stage, and the mere sight of him decides the question.

FERGAN. You are right. I cannot harm him. It will be enough if I teach myself not to love him. *(decisively)* You will take him away. You will start at once with him.

IRENE. I will not start.

FERGAN. What?

IRENE. I will not consent to be thrust out of doors. For my son's sake I will sacrifice nothing of his regular position, of the consideration attaching to his legal birth.

FERGAN. Then I shall force you.

IRENE. No.

FERGAN. The divorce that you were so anxious for, I now wish for and demand.

IRENE. I no longer accept it. My youth is past; my hopes are dead; my woman's future is at an end. I refuse to change the whole course of my life. I wish for nothing more than to remain to the end where I am—as I am.

FERGAN. You want me to put up with you?

IRENE. You must! You have nothing against me but my own confession.

However he revolts, he still protests. What, a whole life together face to face, always, always? What sort of existence will he lead? And she answers, "The same that I have led for ten years." " But," he cries, " you are guilty and I am innocent." " No, we are only two miserable people, and misery knows none but equals."

La Loi de l' Homme, played during the winter of 1897 at the Comédie Française, has much affinity with *Les Tenailles*. The same concentration, the same severity of style, the same contempt of petty devices. Like *Les Tenailles*, *La Loi de l' Homme* is a violent attack upon the law with regard to marriage and divorce. Like *Les Tenailles*, *La Loi de l' Homme* consists of two situations, which are opposed, or, to speak more exactly, of one and the same situation reversed. In the first act the wife is at the mercy of the husband ; in the third the husband must surrender to the wife. Only the first of these two plays gave the mind the same kind of satisfaction which arises from a neat proposition followed by its contrary, or from a well-worked out algebraical equation. The same law furnished the key with which the former prisoner locked up her jailor. In the new play, the law, as conceived and framed by men, the same law which furnished Irene Fergan, the adulteress, with so excellent a retort, can do nothing to give freedom to Laure de Raguais, who is an honest woman. Deceived by her husband, she has discovered in his writing-desk some conclusive letters, and she learns from the very lips of the representative of authority that these letters can do nothing for her. She wants to have the lovers surprised, but she shrinks back from the stupid and ignoble formalities with which the law has surrounded the proof of *le flagrant délit* when it is a question of masculine infidelity. Consequently, she must content herself with an amicable separation. She will have the shame of remaining the wife of an adulterer, and the grief of feeling that he has a share in her daughter. As for him, he will keep his mistress.

The years pass. Little Isabelle de Raguais has grown up. She in her turn loves and is loved. André d'Orcien would be worthy of her, but his mother is the mistress of M. de Raguais. Imagine the disgust, the supreme revolt of the poor mother, who seems to see her daughter torn away from her and given to the woman who has already robbed her of her husband. Will she consent to one of those hideous compromises which oblige the victim and the executioner to live side by side in the same family ? Impossible. Here, again, M. de Raguais has an ally in the law, always the law of man ! He can virtually ignore his wife's wishes and disregard her veto. But M. d'Orcien and his son, André, are men of honour and men of heart, and the idea of forcing themselves into a family, or of a daughter marrying against her mother's wishes, is alien to their private code. M. d'Orcien insists on seeing Madame de Raguais in the presence of his own wife and of M. de Raguais. He must have a free consent, or a refusal with reasons given. Here is Madame. de Raguais' opportunity for vengeance ; she will tell the truth to the injured husband, and force a confession from the guilty pair.

Is she right, or is she wrong ? That question was discussed over the sweetmeats at all the five o'clock teas of Paris, which gave me occasion to remark that the *esprit de corps*, formerly so powerful among women, is a thing of the past. Some threw Laure de Raguais overboard out of cowardice, to please the lord and master, to whom they had decided to show indulgence at all costs. Others, on the contrary, abandoned her in the name of the maternal affection which Laure sacrificed to her vengeance ; and others, because they were wily birds, full of resource and armed at all points for the struggle, so that with or without the law of man they had a thousand ways of slipping off the yoke under which Paul Hervieu's heroine succumbed. There are blundering, stupid women, and Madame de Raguais was one of them ; she did not know how to make herself loved; she did not know how to make herself obeyed. She had nothing on her side, as she said herself, but her "tears and her claws." She made use of them ; she did well. Why pardon the guilty, who remain un-repentant in their crimes ?

But I come back to the play. The situation is now in the hands of M. d'Orcien, who in a few seconds, and under our very eyes, has to pass through all the phases of an evolution which would require long hours, weeks, months, per-haps years. But this concentration of psycho-logical development is the distinctive, permanent, and inevitable condition of the stage. Call it a convention, if you will; but it is a convention which is the very life of tragedy. Consequently, M. d'Orcien, though he gives way at first to an alarming outburst of anger, grows calmer when he thinks of his son, the only being whom he can still love. In the name of André and Isabelle, those two innocent creatures whose hearts and lives would be broken by an exposure, he proposes, or rather he insists, since he has the right to insist, that there shall be silence, peace, oblivion. Clearly there can be no question here of drinking champagne and forming one single household, as at the end of *La Sérénade*. If M. Hervieu had dreamed of anything so brutal, I should never have forgiven him, and I should never have forgiven myself for taking his play seriously. But nothing of the sort happens. The great world, like the world of diplomacy, knows how to bring about reconciliations which are not intimacies, and if some silences are base, others are heroic.

I will not allow that *La Loi de l'Homme* is much inferior to *Les Tenailles*. I am infinitely more interested in Laure de Raguais, who is only a silly woman, than in Irene Fergan, who is a very decided minx. The solution of *La Loi de l'Homme* is much less neat than that of *Les Tenailles*, but it is more human; and for my part I should be disposed to like the piece just because of that dénouement which has been so much criticised. But M. Hervieu does not care to have his pieces liked. They make no attempt to win sympathy, indeed, they rather repel it. They plunge us into lamentable situations, yet we do not shed a single tear. The writers of an older generation observed, M. Hervieu experiments. What do I mean by experimenting? I mean observation in specially chosen conditions prepared beforehand—isolation, so to speak, of the psychological phenomenon from the thousand circumstances which might obstruct it, or falsify it, or complicate it. So he imitates the physicist, who studies the fall of bodies in a void so as to arrive at the true laws of gravity and attraction; or the naturalist, who binds up the muscle in a rabbit so as to observe the separate action either of the motor apparatus or the apparatus of sensibility.   That is to say, he practises abstraction, or science, no longer as a matter of reasoning, but as a matter of practice.

M. Hervieu thereby condemns himself to loss of imagination and of wit.   He deprives himself of the aid of rhetoric and of poetry.   Psychology itself gives him nothing but a starting point, it does not give him characters.   The secondary figures are nothing but shadows, and as to those which move in the foreground, they have only one sentiment and one attitude.   Apart from their position as husband and wife, they are anything you like.   They can only be realised by an effort like that required to conceive points without dimensions, surfaces without thickness, or bodies without weight.   It is a hard, uncompromising kind of art, born of weariness and giving birth to it.   M. Hervieu goes straight on, dragging us behind him; he never stops to gather a flower by the way.   He will neither accept nor seek for those happy turns of expression which made Dumas and Augier such delightful companions.   No; he seems to despise anything like naturalness in dialogue, although, after all, there is nothing wrong in it. However poor, limited, stiff, his vocabulary may be, he insists on making it poorer, stiffer, more contracted—he positively revels in it. In spite of the force of his ideas, and the soundness of his thesis, will the public ever be on familiar terms with these gloomy plays, this anatomy of the drama? Certainly a biological experiment has an interest of its own, but to feel pleasure one must be presented with life itself. Now this is exactly what M. Maurice Donnay has once or twice succeeded in presenting.

The first actors at his disposal were some Chinese shadow dancers at the Chat Noir. These *artistes*, cut out in tin, had a definite influence on M. Donnay's dramatic career. They accustomed him to dare and say anything. At the Chat Noir he had a show represented called *Ailleurs*, which did not spare our public men or our institutions, and also a little archaic burlesque, *Phryne*, which was played in February, 1891, but was not printed until 1894, with a dedication to *feu Patin*. Patin, good honest man, was in his time a Professor at the

Sorbonne, Perpetual Secretary to the Académie Française, and the author of the *Tragiques Grecs.* Would he have accepted this *enfant terrible,* who claimed him as a parent—this rather unexpected and compromising pupil, who descended upon him from Montmartre? He is now in a world which I have every reason to believe a better world, since it is impossible to imagine a worse one than this. Consequently, the answer to the question belongs exclusively to the domain of table-rapping and automatic letter writing. But I am inclined to think that if he had read *Phryne,* the few hairs that he had when I knew him would have stood straight up on his bald and polished yellow pate.

M. Donnay kept to the same vein in writing *Lysistrata,* which is a very free adaptation of the *Ecclesiazousai* and the *Eirene* of Aristophanes. This time, instead of a luminous circle on a piece of white calico, M. Donnay could disport himself on the vast stage of the *Vaudeville,* and, in place of punched-out silhouettes, it was interpreted by beautiful girls, beautifully dressed. The transparency of the muslin would of itself have attracted the crowd; but M. Donnay added words worse than muslin. His work was like the musical burlesques of forty years ago, *Orphée aux Enfers, La Belle Hélène,* or the burlesques of Burnand and Byron, in so far as it put very modern sentiments into the mouths of antique characters. When the sentimental courtesan prefaces her false confidences by the words, " Daughter of a superior officer," . . . or when we see the snobs of Athens having their linen washed at Corinth, just as Bourget's Parisians send theirs to London, we have in an accentuated degree the vulgar kind of comedy that gives you Plato hailing an omnibus for the Gates of Hell, or Jupiter calling out to Ixion, whose palace is on fire, " Are you insured?" But *Lysistrata* differs from these ancient farces in not being a parody. It is no attack upon heroic literature or heroic art. It contents itself with grafting Parisian *blague* upon the *blague* of Athens, and, after all, the two are not so very different. The author gets his effects not from the disparity, but from the similarity of manners and sentiments, which is no impossibility. . Moreover, here and there he has given the piece a poetical colouring, just as Aristophanes did, a feat which would have been as difficult for Crémieux and Halévy as for Byron and Burnand. No nation ever equalled the Greeks in the art of describing young, elegant, smiling depravity and adorning sensuality with a thousand graces. That immoral, delightful form of art we once possessed and then lost. M. Donnay learnt it from the Greeks by the aid of Patin, and has restored it to us again.

The young author completed his course of irony at the Chat Noir. At the same time, like all the Frenchmen of his age, he must have noted the movement of the Théâtre Libre, although he does not seem to have written any play for M. Antoine. Without committing himself to any system or counter system, he picked up by the way certain ideas which accorded with his kind of wit. For example, that life is a sort of mystification. We live for the most part in full comedy; now and again we rise to serious drama; then we relapse into comedy, or, at least, to the realm of *terre-à-terre*, everyday material, mechanical existence, where every sky is dull and grey. His three modern plays, *Pension de Famille*, *Amants*, and *La Douloureuse*, follow this type, and unfold their action in the order which I have just indicated. But when the authors of M. Antoine's school tried to prove to him that the best play is a play that is no play, he did not believe a word of it, and reserved to himself the right of being clever when he found an opportunity. He was no less incredulous when he was told that wit is an element fatal to comedy, for he had a good store of that kind of merchandise, and he had every intention of placing it on the market. Above all, he saw quite clearly that the cardinal error of the Théâtre Libre was that of placing sensual love on the stage just at the moment when it was degenerating into a morbid habit, the disease of love, which Stendhal omitted, or, rather, which he justifiably eliminated, from his formal classification. But before it descends to that degenerate level, has it not had its glorious hour of freshness, its springtide of blossom, its share of what we call in France "la beauté du diable "? Immoral, if you please; but pleasant to the eyes for all but Puritans. Will not such a strain command a hearing? The innumerable editions of Pierre Loti answer in the affirmative. This kind of sensualism Loti has depicted with as profound and serious a conviction as if it were a religion, with a wonderful art, breathing all the poetry that is in us and around us, an art that is almost innocent in its ardour and simplicity. Imagine Loti, a child of the Boulevards, and making his début at the Chat Noir; take away his painter's palette, and give him in its place the humour of Gavroche, and you will have something very like Maurice Donnay.

He had only risen to half his proper stature in *Pension de Famille.* The scene was laid in one of those cosmopolitan hotels on the Riviera, the characters were men and women in search of adventure, drawn hither from all parts of the world in the hope of stimulating their worn-out nerves by some new freak of fancy. The events were merely some trifling incidents of the *table d'hôte.* Then in the midst of this atmosphere, which gradually becomes charged with amorous electricity, there is a sudden explosion, but after all no one is wounded, the scandal miscarries, the revolver misses fire. But whether it is that M. Donnay presumed too much on his skill in handling so many threads at once, or whether the public is weary of these series of types and combinations of petty intrigues, *Pension de Famille* did not have a very long run. To make up for it, *Amants* filled the bills for a long time at the Renaissance, and I know that whenever one mentions this play to a Parisian, his eyes light up with the memory of a vivid, delicious sensation. Each generation has one book which it cherishes tenderly, one play dear above all others, in which the reader, or the spectator, identifies himself with the hero, one work which for ten or fifteen years fixes the language of love. To be young and to discover it, is to be thrown into a fever, and to see it again is to experience a softening of the heart and a gentle melancholy. When at last it gives place to new successes, one feels inclined to say with Mürger's lover, " O ma jeunesse c'est vous que l'on enterre!" I think that *Amants* will be that play, for all who had reached the age of love when it was played, for the lovers on their promotion in 1895. But that number is swelled by so many precocious boys and belated elders.

I said something about the *milieu* of the play, when I was speaking of Jeanne Granier. She played the principal part with Lucien Guitry, who is not unknown in London. When the curtain rises on Claudine Rozay's drawing-room, the representation of " Guignol " has just come to an end. The children and their mammas are delighted, the mammas very elegant, the children dressed in a pronounced English style and under the care of a " Miss " and a " Fräulein," whose efforts to keep them in check are wonderfully ineffective. There is respectability in the air—respectability of a rather artificial and superficial kind. As if to put us off the scent the Prefect of Police is in the drawing-room as an invited guest. However, we begin to sniff a somewhat doubtful odour. We understand by certain phrases that these women are not married, that these children are not children like our own, and that the Prefect has come to amuse himself.

In fact, this is the demi-monde, the world of sham *ménages*, temporary fidelity, and virtue for a season. To give us a picture of these *femmes entretenues*, struggling to live like excellent *bourgeoises* is in itself piquant, it becomes still more piquant when we turn to society nowadays and see a crowd of silly excitable women, whose longing for Bohemianism leads them into a hundred follies.

Here M. Donnay has employed the same device used by Arthur Pinero in that masterpiece of the present English stage, *The Second Mrs. Tanqueray*. Just as Paula is more or less repeated and parodied by Lady Orreyd, who represents the absurdities and vulgarities of the married courtesan, the supernumeraries in *Amants* are left to bring out clearly the practical, domesticated courtesan, the *courtisane popote*, who knows how to look after her tradesmen, keep her accounts, and educate her children. We feel that for all Claudine's greater delicacy of mind, she sees life after all, just as these women see it. Hidden away in the bottom of her heart there is something of the man of busi·

ness. Like all Parisian women she is a born arithmetician, and with it all she is kind, she would not make any one suffer; she adores her child, and she cherishes an attachment for its father, which is the result of habit, gratitude, sympathy, and I shall add respect, if the word may be forgiven. Yes, but she can love, and although she knows very well what that leads to, she has not the strength to turn her back upon it, or to be vexed, when she hears the first notes of the music. From the very beginning, although she makes a show of resistance for form's sake, we know that she will not repulse Véthenil. One wonders what will happen. Will they be denounced, will they be surprised? Doubtless there will be another woman, jealousy, a duel, someone will kill someone else, perhaps every one will die. You are quite mistaken: they will not be denounced; they will not be surprised; they will be jealous, but as usual, jealous for no reason at all, or for absurd reasons which can only end in those thousand little no-things that make up the history of love. Nothing will happen, and no one will die. Someone will marry someone else, but it will not be Véthenil who marries Claudine.

The whole play is nothing but the history of a *liaison*, the evolution of love. First act: they meet; they like each other; they flirt; they discuss the love which the one does not wish to feel, and the other feels already. Second act: they are in love; they talk nonsense; they quarrel and make it up again. Third act: they are still in love; they break with one another; they suffer; they come together again. Fourth act: their love is stronger and deeper, yet they separate with a great rending of hearts, which is in itself supreme happiness. Verily this fourth act is dangerous to see and hear; it is the paroxysm, the acute crisis, the heroic moment when any sacrifice, any madness seems possible. Claudine, for all her prudence, is ready to forget everything—rest, future, fortune, even her child. Those passionate farewells, this solitude, this Italian night, this nature made for love is all too much for nerves strung to breaking point. The man is wiser, perhaps because a suspicion of melancholy satiety is already to be felt in his wisdom. What separates them finally? A *coup de théâtre?* No, simply the coachman. "If monsieur does not wish to miss the train, he has only just time." In the fifth act they meet again, but cured, and they philosophise gently, sadly, tenderly over the past.

Is there nothing but love, then, in the play? There is everything, a whole crowd of things, when one comes to think of it. Francueil's journey; the history of two pastrycooks, the false Alexandrine who is the good one, and the true who is the bad one; a discussion about the worthlessness of servants; a toast; a fable in verse, varying from five to twenty-two feet in a line. Princess Soukhimiliki and her music-hall songs; a receipt for making "cocktail"; an anecdote about an Irishwoman, who belonged to an orchestra of Hungarian ladies, and was the mistress of the Siamese ambassador; a whole host of things, which do not serve the action of the piece. And that is the reason why M. Donnay has thrust them into his play. If these details did serve the action of the play, he would be taking a leaf out of Scribe's book or Sardou's, and they are hopelessly out of date.

As to the sentiments of Claudine and Véthenil, we can follow without a shadow of effort their capricious and yet fatal development. They deal in self-analysis, whilst all the time laughing at "that confounded mania for self-analysis which possesses us." But their psychology is never pedantic or emphatic. The only reproach that can be brought against them is that sometimes they are too subtle and too witty. Here is a characteristic fragment. Claudine is scolding Véthenil very prettily for his ill-humour, which springs from his secret jealousy of the lover *en titre*. "If *you* are disagreeable, you must not be angry with *me*, it is not *his* fault." Note the mischief hidden in these three possessive pronouns, which I have emphasised. M. Donnay's style is loose, somewhat disordered, but it is an elegant disorder, like that of a pretty woman who has put on a peignoir to be more at her ease, but who is not the less pretty for that—quite the contrary. M. Donnay's careless, fantastic method contains, perhaps, not very much art, but, at all events, much artistic instinct. He is more of a literary artist than any of our other dramatic authors, Lavedan, perhaps, being bracketed equal, and Lemaître, of course, *hors concours.*

Many writers are capable only of one single work, into which they put their whole soul, all their talents, all their invention, till there is nothing left. People asked, some anxiously, others hopefully, if by chance *Amants* would not be M. Donnay's only play. *La Douloureuse,* which I saw in 1897, has not altogether dispelled the anxiety of M. Donnay's admirers, but neither has it altogether contradicted the hopes of his rivals. It is a badly-constructed, ill-conceived play, with some parts of the highest merit. The first act forms a play by itself. It is a light-heartedly cruel picture of the " Panama Group," and its different states of mind. We have an outpouring of alarming cynicism, and also an exhibition of four little girls, singing, dancing, twirling and what not. Then the officers come to arrest M. Ardan, the banker, who is giving a party that evening according to the immemorial custom of bankers, ready to take the final leap.

He asks to go into his dressing room, and there blows out his brains. The thing is whispered in the drawing-room, but supper is served, and, *ma foi*, the world sups.

In the second act the play begins. No, not yet; first of all we must join in the discussion as to whether a woman, deceived by the man she loves, ought to resent it, or to pardon it. The Second Empire, represented by Madame Leformal, debates the question with the Third Republic, personified in Hélène Ardan. Apparently the wife of the Second Empire overlooked everything in her husband, only she forgot to instil religious principles into her children, and without religion there is no resignation. This is why the daughter of this indulgent mother is an out-and-out rebel. In the fourth act, be it observed, she will prove as forgiving as her mother, whence it follows that all this comparative psychology of the two generations means nothing at all. It is a complete absurdity, and we must go to the *Vaudeville* of 1897 to learn that the *cocodettes* of 1867 were " bénisseuses." In any case, they were not fools, and I can assure M. Donnay that they would make short work of the champions of the new generation in less time than it takes me to write it.

At last all these people go off. I take out my watch. It is a quarter past ten, and the real play was just about to begin. Hèlène Ardan, whose husband paid his debts with a couple of ounces of powder, has been for a long time in love with Philippe Lamberty. She is only waiting for the end of her widowhood to marry him. It is a fatal delay, for it allows Gotte des Trembles, who is bored by her husband's neglect, to make a dead set at Philippe. They are in the garden one evening; Gotte is pretty and disturbing, because she herself is disturbed. Philippe is a man. I am in a desperate fright, but suddenly Philippe pulls himself together and explains to the poor little goose how base it would be to deceive her friend, the noble Hélène, so happy, so devoted, so trusting. And the poor little goose thanks the moralist effusively.

I do not know, my dear sir, if you ever found yourself alone in a park at sunset with a young woman whose wrists burnt your fingers, and

whose ideas of duty were getting into a mist. I
am quite sure that in that case you also preached
her a little sermon. And what happened then ?
One of two things. Either you went away, and
the little woman for the rest of your natural life
was your mortal, irreconcilable enemy, or you
stayed, and the temptation was renewed on the
next day, until you succumbed. Philippe chose
the second alternative, or rather, we have first
one, then the other. Gotte triumphs, but only
for an instant. Philippe is horror-struck at his
own downfall, and with the cowardice which
characterises our sex, he lets his accomplice feel
this. Then Gotte revenges herself by revealing
to Philippe that Hélène had another lover before
him. That confidence has the foreseen and
desired effect. Philippe, the culprit, poses as
the victim, the avenger, whilst Hélène is crushed
to the earth by his reproaches. But how did he
guess, how did he know ? One person only
could have told him—Gotte ! In a lightning
flash Hélène has understood. What, at the very
moment when he was faithless to her, he is
overwhelming her with his jealousy and his

contempt. " Now, really, that is funny, too funny." And when they have said everything insulting, heart-rending, cruel that they can think of, they stand looking at one another, haggard, broken. How will this terrible scene end? Just as it would end in real life. "What time is it after all this?" murmurs Hélène, as if awakening from a dream. "Seven o'clock, and I am dining out! I shall look pretty! (*Going up to the glass and speaking very low.*) Ah, my head! (*Arranging her hair and putting on her hat with convulsive, feverish fingers. He wraps her cloak around her shoulders. They look at one another.*) Who is that coming in? André? I do not want to see him." *Philippe.* "Then go out through the studio." And she goes out without a word. How many men and women among the audience can recall similar scenes in their secret history which ended very much like that! Strictly speaking, the play might have ended there, but M. Donnay insists on showing us the two lovers reconciled, softened, happy. Only to reach that result he thought that he must transport them far from

Paris to the blue shore of the Mediterranean. The scene of *Pension de Famille* was laid in a suburb of Nice; and in the fourth act of *Amants* we were on the shore of an Italian lake; whilst the fourth act of *La Douloureuse* takes us to the pines of Cap Martin. We cannot but take note of that irresistible instinct to call in nature as an ally, and to turn to those sunny lands where life is easier and love more indulgent. However, M. Donnay must take care; he is too fond of travelling over the line of the P.L.M.; next time, perhaps, the public may take umbrage.

What is there in the fourth act? Absolutely nothing. M. Donnay has stuffed it full of useless things, some of them in very bad taste. The act might have been written in one single sentence. "We are not worth very much, let us forgive one another; let us love one another, and let us try not to yield to temptation." Moreover, that sentence sums up the whole philosophy of M. Donnay, and, I fear, the whole morality of his age.

It is all very well to talk about expiation.

La Douloureuse reminds one of the bill that the waiter offers you at the end of a good dinner. We saw how Gaston Ardan paid his bill with a pistol shot, but did that pistol shot compensate the people whom he had ruined? Gotte's bad behaviour was largely due to the systematic neglect and infidelity of her husband, but I do not see that he was punished. As for Philippe, his expiation consists of two months' solitude at Cap Martin, which is a pleasant enough form of penance. I cannot forbear to notice the unpardonable recklessness with which the author in the last act drags in the name of an illustrious and revered Princess to support his doctrine of expiation. She, Monsieur, only paid for the crimes and follies of others, and that, I think, is the final condemnation of this pretended justice of fate.

"Do not let us bring suffering upon those that love us." In the general shipwreck of creeds and principles that is the only thing left to guide M. Donnay's heroes through life; all beyond is doubt and darkness. There is nothing good except joy, nothing evil except suffering. When M. Donnay wrote that line in *Phryne*, which assuredly does not smack of the midnight oil—

"Hélas! Eros nous mène, et rien ne prouve rien"—

he was giving utterance all unconsciously to a whole philosophy, a complete conception of life. I see no sign that he has changed.

I might add other names to the list of new writers whose work I have been studying in some detail. M. Gustave Guichet, for example; M. Guimon; M. de Porto-Riche, the author of *Le Passé;* M. Abel Hermant, a clever and forcible novelist, who produced *La Meute* for the Renaissance, and more recently *La Carrière* and *Les Transatlantiques* for the Gymnase; M. Pierre Valdagne, who made his début at the Théâtre Libre, and has since appeared at the Odéon, in *La Blague;* others besides who show evidence of talent, and who are trying to shake off the tyranny of old formulas. But I do not think that any of them would furnish me with characters which I have not already observed amongst the writers at this moment in the first rank. They would not add anything to the provisional definition of what I have called, after M. Faguet, M. Larroumet, and others, the "new comedy." I said just now "provisional definition," and I know that these two words are at open war with one another. I also feel how difficult it is to include under the same definition, literary temperaments, as diverse as Lemaître and Brieux, Hervieu and Donnay seem to be at first sight. But if we hesitated to define life we should never define anything, since everything lives and moves, everything is progressing and advancing. The very diversity of mankind helps the critic instead of embarrassing him. For the very fact that they have many points of contact and agreement shows him that all are driven by the same wind, and forced to converge by the same intellectual current.

This is what I seem to see.

Let us first of all consider the construction of plays. Intrigue is simplified and reduced to a minimum. Instead of "placing" the characters upon the stage, the first act is employed in explaining the *milieu*, the setting of the action. If this description is unnecessary, because the *milieu* is well known to everybody beforehand, the first act sets the action in motion. But the action is nothing except character painting, and instead of this occupying the first act, it now occupies all the acts. So that, as M. Faguet has remarked, we get back to the art of Molière and his immediate successors, that is to say, to living portraits. And when several of these types are grouped before us, we have no longer a portrait but a picture. As for incident, all that does not spring from the play itself and the interplay of character is eliminated, just as all circumstances alien to the phenomenon under observation are eliminated from a scientific experiment. I purposely dwell upon this comparison. The spectator who used to give all his attention to the complexity of the intrigue, now gives it to the psychological complications. His reason is called into play instead of his memory, but he is still obliged to collaborate with the dramatic writer, and necessarily so, for there will never be a real drama without this collaboration. There must still be preparation where preparation is needed, and explanation where explanation is called for, but for the most part the writer confines himself to suggestion. Those witty lookers on who passed judgment upon the play whilst it was in progress, and who embodied the author's ideas, those brilliant *rôles à côté*, which sometimes eclipsed the hero and heroine, have vanished altogether. That is to say, the chorus of antiquity has been banished from the scene, at any rate, until it is fetched back again. But what has become of wit which was formerly so necessary? It is not excluded, but it is no longer *de rigueur*. It still figures in the menu of the evening, but only as a *hors d'œuvre*, or as a condiment. Love has once more been granted the licence to be witty that it had lost since the days of Marivaux. As for the dénouement, it must do the best it can. So much the better if it can prove something, so much the worse if it proves nothing. At any rate, in that case it will prove that the author has made a bad choice, for all good subjects lead up of themselves to a conclusion. The only thing absolutely forbidden is that the author should interfere. No *coup de théâtre,* no *deus ex machina,* no intervention of fortune, no chastisement falling from Heaven, nothing that can suggest a farce or a melodrama. Thereby we are conforming to the æsthetic principles of the Théâtre Libre, but in all other points we are leaving it behind and drawing closer to the old dramatic architecture, which prevailed from 1830 to 1880. For example, we have preserved the *péripétie,* that is to say, towards eleven o'clock, or a quarter-past eleven, at the end of the penultimate act, the action comes to a crisis and we reach the high-water-mark of emotion. A whisper goes through the audience: "How on earth will they get out of it?" and here peeps out the little finger of Scribe.

Such is the new, or more or less new comedy, a slightly hybrid and bastard variety, which the professors are beginning to patronise, because they have been assured that it is only a revival of the "comedy of character" associated with Molière, and therefore, in their eyes, the highest expression of dramatic art. Some of them believe it, others pretend to believe it. At any

rate, this form has the merit of being very wide
and elastic.   You can put into it what you like.
M. Hervieu and M. Brieux have fitted a problem
play into it; M. Donnay a sensual novel; M.
Lavedan a picture of manners, a social study ; M.
Lemaître, his dramatic experiences of every kind.
It is not in itself either moral or immoral; it
lends itself to the Attic imagination of Montmartre ; perhaps to-morrow some Puritan may
make it a vehicle for a sermon.   Reactionary,
bourgeois, anarchist, it is capable of anything.
Even from a purely artistic point of view its
tendencies are not yet clearly defined.   It is only
masterpieces that fix a style and make it definite.
Then, but only then, the form will be perfect and
nothing more can be done but break it up to
make new ones, and so deliver the masterpieces
from that fate, at once the cruellest degradation
and the height of glory, cheap and unlimited
reproduction.

VII.

THE REVIVAL OF VERSE ON THE STAGE.

I HAVE tried to indicate the new tendencies which have come to light during the last five or six years in comedy proper, and the authors who are its principal exponents. Throughout the period, melodrama and vaudeville have remained pretty nearly at a standstill. There is no need, I think, to give English readers any account of our melodramas. Many of them still cross the Channel: they are amongst the wares which we manufacture and export with some success. But in France melodrama seems to be losing ground. It still holds the field at L'Ambigu and the Théâtre de la République; but it has lost the Gaîté, and only makes an intermittent appearance at the Châtelet and the Porte Saint Martin. It has not forsaken the ancient tracks, and I have never heard that M. Decourcelle, the author of

Les Deux Gosses, treats the methods and productions of M. d'Ennery, the author of *Les Deux Orphelines*, with the contempt evinced for Scribe and Sardou by neophytes in other branches of the drama. Clearly there has been some evolution even in melodrama. Up to the middle of the century characters, situations, style, *mise-en-scène* belonged alike to the realm of fancy. But the melodrama of to-day is half idealist, half realist, that is to say it consists of vulgarity and impossibility in nearly equal proportions. No sort of observation in the moral delineation of the characters, good or bad; no suspicion of probability in the procession of events; but a scrupulous imitation of life in dialogue, in scenery, in all the accessories of the *mise-en-scène.* In short, the old style of the Martainvilles and Pixérécourts has vanished, but the system remains intact.

The same want of movement appears in the vaudeville and all its numerous sub-varieties. This word "vaudeville" is deceptive. Formerly it signified a play interspersed with rhyming couplets, scarcely differing from the modern operetta; now it includes all that the English mean by a word which has a very clear and definite signification, "farce." Labiche and Meilhac had done much for that inferior kind of play. The one based it upon a thoroughly sound observation of human nature and conduct amongst the middle classes; the second found a mine of wealth in the world of pleasure. They have had numberless successors: Alexandre Bisson, the author of *Le Lycée de jeunes filles, Le Député de Bombignac, La Famille Pontbiquet*, Paul Ferrier, Albin Valabrègue, Maurice Desvallières, George Feydeau, Léon Gaudillot, as well as the younger comic writers brought to light by the Théâtre Libre, George Ancey and Courteline, the lucky author of *Boubouroche*. Thanks to their efforts, France and the nations dealing in French markets, are assured of a laugh at any rate for some time to come. These gentlemen have plenty of wits, but a thirst for novelty does not seem to trouble them. The innocent young girl, who moves through the most doubtful situations without so much as perceiving them, the serious gentleman who goes in for dissipation on the sly, adultery approached, as Molière approached it, from its grotesque side, electoral platitudes, the meanness of the political world raised to the height of caricature, the new military turn given to French manners by compulsory service, are some of the themes round which the imagination of the Vaudevillistes seems never weary of playing. The deputy and the magistrate are frequently their victims, but their favourite butt is the mother-in-law, whether tyrannical or sentimental. She it is for whom they reserve the most biting of their epigrams, not from any motive of personal vengeance, nor even from comic instinct, but out of pure respect for tradition. It has been understood in France for several centuries that husbands, doctors, and mothers-in-law are proper objects of ridicule.

The canvas of the play is as invariable as the types themselves. The farce is composed according to certain rules, very much like the cookery recipes of the *cuisinière bourgeoise*. First, a good definite misunderstanding, or even two, or three, so that by the end of the last act but one everything is turned topsy-turvey, and not a soul can distinguish his left hand from his right. The whole secret of this kind of play lies in a nutshell; someone is hunting for something from eight o'clock till midnight and must on no account find the person or object of his search until five minutes to twelve. The ideal farce makes the hunted individual be himself looking for another individual, who pursues a third, who is chasing a fourth, and so on, until the last is left trying to catch up the first, which completes the circle and gives an unlimited acceleration of speed to the gyrations of the play. Even with the inevitable five doors, one room no longer suffices. We must have a house with several stories, staircases, roofs, balconies, to give room for this curious chase. You have seen *A Night Out*, which is the last effort of the French genius in this line. I admire these beautiful productions, as indeed I ought; but I am obliged to confess that we have got back to the memorable *Chapeau de paille d'Italie*, and have thereby lost the whole advance made by Labiche and Meilhac. There were some touches worthy of Labruyère in *Célimare le bien aimé* and in *Le Voyage de Perrichon;* the first act of *La Cagnotte* was a chapter from Balzac; whilst *Les Curieuses* was like an instantaneous photograph, stereotyping both the language and manners of the *cocodettes* of 1867. What can anyone find in the farces of our own day except a sort of artificial merriment manufactured by mechanical processes out of materials which have already been used, much as you make white paper out of waste paper. Ill betide a man imprudent enough to seek for information about our moral and social condition!

I can imagine a learned lecturer of Borneo or Tahiti, in the year 4000 after Christ, prefacing his remarks on *La Famille Pontbiquet* somewhat in this fashion. It will be included that year with the *Miles Gloriosus* and the *Ecclesiazousai* in the B.A. course, for looking down the centuries, Bisson would appear first cousin to Aristophanes and Plautus. " Gentlemen," he will say, "we see by *La Famille Pontbiquet*, that at the end of the nineteenth century, the professors of the Lycée Charlemagne at Paris, had mistresses amongst the actresses of the Folies Bergère; and when these ladies were themselves hanging to a trapeze, they picked up a man by his waist-belt between their teeth, and made him whirl round in this position two hundred times a minute." From this fact he will proceed with admirable logic to deduce the character of the intellectual and moral education received at the Lycée Charlemagne. Perhaps, in the meanwhile, you will feel tempted to do the same.

An attempt has recently been made to revive pantomime, not the stupid magnificent spectacle which invades half the London theatres towards Christmas, and puts literature to flight, but the true pantomime—for here the French tongue has the advantage, both in clearness and etymology—the drama in which not a word is spoken, but the meaning is conveyed by facial movement, glance, attitude, or gesture. It is the most artistic of all kinds of acting, and, even though mute, one of the most literary because one of the most suggestive. It requires the greatest amount of reflection and the truest inspiration, as well as cleverness, patience, and taste in the highest degree. This pantomime, once so dear to Gautier and Banville, has fallen into disuse since the disappearance of the great mimics Kalpestri, Paul Legrand, and the immortal Deburau, whose floury hand I had the honour of shaking thirty years ago, when I was dramatic critic at Grenoble. A young girl, Felicia Mallet, tried to use the marvellous flexibility of her face and figure in the revival of pantomime. She gained much applause, but the art which she cultivated so successfully has not a large enough *clientèle* to fill a theatre for any length of time. One cannot live on pantomime, and Felicia Mallet changed her trade, like the grasshopper in the fable. Nowadays she understudies Yvette Guilbert.

I have spoken of the stupid magnificent English pantomime. For an equivalent to its stupidity and magnificence we must go to our old *Féerie*. Poor *Féerie!* It is in a very bad way. One evening last winter I was crossing the Place du Châtelet. It was dark, almost deserted, and swept by the storm. Some men, sheltering in a café, rushed out upon me. They were ticket-mongers, and they offered me a stall at such an extraordinarily low price, and implored me to buy it in such despairing tones, that I must have had either a very lean purse or a very hard heart to resist them. I wonder whether I could not have got my stall for nothing if I had held out a little longer. However I gave way, and I assisted at a few scenes from *La Biche au Bois.* I saw once more the indulgent king and his imbecile major-domo, the charming princess and her faithful Giroflée, the queen Aïka and her minister, the terrible Mesrour. I also saw the warriors in silver helmets shining under the electric light, and the fairies, with their tunics slit up on the left hip and their right arms outstretched, striking attitudes and mouthing their utterances with the most melodramatic modulations. They were no longer the same women (the fairies of my youth must by now be *concierges* or nurses), but they had the same smile, they uttered the same idiotic jests, together with a few new ones not less idiotic, and they sang the same silly words although the tunes were new. I should have fallen asleep, if the cold of the great empty theatre had not kept me awake. Before ten o'clock, I sought my couch, without waiting for the unfortunate princess to recover human form.

It has been said " What is to hinder us from putting new life into the *Féerie* by introducing passion, poetry, real wit and real music ? "   The man who said this was a man of taste and talent, called M. Albert Carré.   He is an actor, an author, and a theatrical manager ;   since the death of Carvalho, he has directed the Opéra Comique, and he was formerly associated with M. Porel in the direction of the Gymnase and the Vaudeville.   He seemed to have everything in his favour, and he had taken care to accumulate on his side all the chances that a skilled man can command.   *La Montagne Enchantée* was played last summer at the Porte Saint Martin ; but it was not a success.

Amongst the extra-literary productions—I had almost said anti-literary—the *Revue* is the most successful.   It first saw the light in 1840, and has gone on flourishing ever since.   It subsists upon two things : indecency and actuality. You cannot call it drama, it is merely journalism in dialogue and action, only journalism studiously divested of everything novel or serious. Not only do all the *Revues* of the same year resemble each other, which would be quite natural, but all the *Revues* of all years are just alike, which is very curious. For it means that every year, whether fateful, glorious, or insignificant, the year of a comet or of a revolution, of a victory or a defeat, of an exhibition or of the cholera, must furnish the same quantity of gaiety and the same number of jests, couplets, and clownish tricks. If the manufacturer of a *Revue* attacks serious matters such as labour disputes, anti-Semitism, or the emancipation of women, it is only to produce comic effects, which would not arise naturally out of these questions. There are some years so full of mournful events and delicate problems, that they afford no subject at all. Then he takes refuge in nonsense, which is why the *Revues* of 1896 and 1897 seemed to me exactly like those that I used to see when I was a schoolboy. For the Russian alliance read the English alliance; for Colonial expansion, free trade, and you have the whole difference. But a *Revue*, like a *Féerie*, is no fit subject for criticism.

'If the public is content, there is nothing more to be said.

After all, the evil is not very great. Since there can be no question of literature in such a connection, neither the decay of the *Féerie*, nor the hopeless mediocrity and the incurable insignificance of the *Revue* need disturb us very much. There is something much sadder and more interesting in the bankruptcy of two kinds of plays, which, in the seventeenth and nineteenth centuries, formed a notable part of our intellectual wealth—I mean tragedy and the poetical drama. Speaking of the stage traditions which prevail at the Théâtre Français, I ventured to remark that the excellent actors of the Maison played Hugo and Racine in the same style and according to the same methods. In their eyes, as well as in the eyes of the public, and even of the authors, the line of demarcation between tragedy and romantic drama has disappeared. Both are plays in verse containing parts for Mounet Sully: contemporary ignorance knows no more, and does not care to ask.

Nevertheless classical tragedy and romantic

drama are essentially incapable of fusion, for tragedy is a thing apart which was brought to perfection two centuries ago, and which it would be more prudent not to touch. It was admirably adapted to the intellectual faculties and requirements of those days. With us it is out of place, and we are not at home in it. A tragedy is neither a poetical conception nor an imitation of real life. It is a moral theorem starting from certain psychological bases, and moving rigorously towards a conclusion. Not that it is beyond the realm of truth; one cannot get outside truth. On the contrary, it draws its material from the most intimate sentiments of the heart, but viewed as a geometrician views ·points, lines, surfaces, and cubic contents. So that a tragic hero resembles ourselves just about as much as an ideal cube resembles a biscuit tin. Classical tragedy, like geometry, admits of no approximations; it must be either perfect or ridiculous. It must needs be a masterpiece in two senses, a triumph of logic in its subject, and of eloquence in its form.

In the poetic drama, on the contrary, the first

necessity is freedom of inspiration; the premises may be false, and the conclusion either absent or unreasonable, but if it has stirred and fascinated us, it is so far good. The drama draws its very life from caprice, imagination, illusion, and the more it deceives us the better we love it. It does not, like tragedy, give us ideal truth, but nature writ large. Thus, whilst tragedy is the triumph of reason, drama is the triumph of imagination. There is the same difference in the form; tragic verse must be eloquent, dramatic verse ought to be, above all, poetical.

Anyone who accepts my definitions will easily understand why tragedy and drama remain as distinct in the critic's crucible as oil and water poured into the same vase. A few years ago we had, and, I think still have, a writer amongst us who devotes himself to tragedy. His name is Alexandre Parodi, and he used to be seen drinking his *mazagran* at the café of the Théâtre Français. *Rome Sauvée* was a real tragedy, and as such had a real success; but I do not know that this success led to anything except parodies of Parodi: certainly the author himself never succeeded in repeating his first inspiration. Last summer we had a *Frédégonde* at the Théâtre Français, the work of M. Dubout, a banker of Boulogne-sur Mer. It may be noted as a characteristic fact that to write a tragedy in 1897, one must needs be a banker. Did not the school of Pope amongst you come to an end with a banker? When tragedy no longer affords poets a living, it is itself driven to live upon bankers. The theatres, which lend themselves to these attempts, are not exactly flourishing, as was attested by the financial report lately submitted to the Sociétaires of the Rue Richelieu. This report confirms the sad results of *Frédégonde* upon the receipts, and such a confirmation is not without its critical value. M. Dubout brought an action against M. Lemaître for having said in print that his play was badly constructed. He should have brought another against M. Claretie for having confessed that it cost more than it brought in.

This is the leading situation in M. Dubout's play. Frédégonde has come to confess to Bishop Prétextat, but her confession is an act of sacrilege and bravado. She reveals both her past and future crimes; she tells him what means she is taking to insure the death of the young Mérovée, her enemy and son-in-law. Prétextat longs to prevent this assassination, but can only do so by violating the secret of the confessional. The man in him awakes under the priest's frock, and he is impelled to put an end to the wretched woman with his own hands, even in the holy place. He would have yielded to the temptation, had not the chant of the Miserere, rising and falling in the depths of the church, reminded him that he is the minister of the God who said "Thou shalt not kill." This situation is more violent than really strong. It is not tragedy, it is melodrama. In reality *Frédégonde* is only a melodrama with literary pretensions, taken haphazard from the famous *Récits* of Augustin Thierry.

There is nothing more painful for a sick man who might be cured, than to be linked with a corpse, whose resuscitation is hopeless. The first thing necessary for the revival of the drama, is its separation from tragedy. But that is not a sufficient remedy, or rather it is no remedy at all, for it merely attributes to the drama the purely negative merit of not resembling tragedy. Whence shall it draw inspiration? Whence shall it steal the spark destined to kindle it into flame? Many writers have invoked the muse of patriotism; in less than twenty years we have had one Vercingetorix, and several Jeannes d'Arc. As we curse the English, we think of the Prussians, and as we offer our hatred and admiration to a fantastic Julius Cæsar, we see in him the combined incarnation of Moltke and Bismarck. M. Déroulède added to this literature —half memory, half suggestion—a *Bertrand Duguesclin* and a *Mort de Hoche*, which contained one very fine scene. Other writers, following the pure romantic tradition, took refuge in the Middle Ages, with which the poetic drama has, in a sense, identified itself ever since Victor Hugo. The seventeenth century had a profound contempt for the Middle Ages, for the childishness of their chronicles, the coarseness of their *fabliaux*, the platitudes and the incredible tediousness of their romances. Since 1825 we believe, or pretend to believe, that in the Middle Ages the stream of poetry has a never-failing source. This is the only fable of romanticism which has survived its author; nowadays it is one of our dearest delusions, one of our *idola fori*, as Bacon would have said. There are two kinds of Mediævalism, the one historical, or semi-historical, and the other a web of mysticism and fable, the age of the Round Table and the Holy Grail. The first gave M. de Bornier his *Fille de Roland*, M. Armand Silvestre plunged into the second, and brought back his *Tristan de Leonnois*.

Other writers have appealed to the religious sentiment, amongst them three distinguished poets, M. Grandmougin, M. Haraucourt, and M. Edmond Rostand. I shall explain presently who M. Edmond Rostand is. M. Haraucourt is one of our greatest lyrical poets, whose place in the academy would be beside Sully-Prudhomme, and José-Maria de Heredia. He yields to none in the nobility of his thought, the width of his view, the pure music of his versification. His prose also is very fine, and I remember a certain preface of his—the work of a literary artist and a philosopher. He wrote a mystery play of the Passion which was played during Holy Week. M. Rostand produced another for the Renaissance, *La Samaritaine*, "a Gospel in three tableaux," which gave complete satisfaction to M. Catulle Mendès. A somewhat disquieting testimony! One would willingly exchange all the qualities in which these gentlemen are so rich, and which, in such a connection, almost amount to faults, for that one single faculty, which sufficed the lowly and simple writers of the true miracle plays, the faculty of faith and of worship. Our poets have not even always possessed reverence and tact.

Another group of writers have invoked Shakespeare. He is the god of M. Catulle Mendès and of M. Emile Bergerat, both men of many gifts (M. Bergerat is the *Caliban* of the *Figaro*), both poets, both sons-in-law of Théophile Gautier, and hence Shakespearians by right of alliance if not of birth. For in the days of Romanticism the cult of Shakespeare was an act of faith, and it is still included in the creed of all who have survived the wreck of the

School. Did not Victor Hugo write, " J'admire tout dans Shakespeare, je l'admire comme une brute " ?

Is this a good plan? I dare not give a decision. Whichever way one looks at it, it is an excellent thing to admire Shakespeare, but to imitate him is another matter. If the fellow-countrymen of the author of *Hamlet* can scarcely succeed, it is hardly probable that he will yield all his secrets to foreigners, and those Neolatins. Many of the aspects of Shakespeare, perhaps the greatest, elude us, and must always elude us. Yet our dramatic writers think that they have imitated Shakespeare, when, forsooth, they have written an irregular, fantastically constructed play, with a multiplicity of intrigue, in which all the characters talk like poets.

There is one literary fiction on which we set great store, because it is very useful for flattering the democracy, and nowadays everyone who courts popularity—whether a minister on his probation, or a budding academician—fawns upon the democracy, just as two centuries ago they would have fawned upon the monarch. I mean the charming idea that poetry has its real dwelling place in the heart of the people. There is nothing more false, and we all know it perfectly. Those who have penetrated to the bottom of this vaunted heart of the people have found nothing but jealousy, malice, and greed. The workman hates both his master and his trade; the peasant loves his land more than his children, he has no eyes for the natural beauty in the midst of which he lives. Beggars are neither philosophers nor poets; for one Villon and one Hégésippe Moreau you can count innumerable idle, cowardly, envious souls who have never conceived one pure or noble thought. Yes, we know all that, but we will not admit it. The workman in cities scarcely allows us any illusions on his account, he takes a cynical pride in exposing his moral degradation. But a little prestige still clings to the peasant; he is so far off and he says so little. One always credits silent people with deep thoughts, ruminating looks so much like dreaming. The peasant, standing mute in the midst of magnificent surroundings, unconsciously borrows dignity from the living poetry that shines round about him, and bathes him in a light that never was on sea or land. That is why we still read *La Mare au Diable, La Petite Fadette, François le Champs*, and all those absolutely fantastic and deceptive books. Take the Virgilian paradox about the man of the fields, and rejuvenate it by a skilful method which I shall presently explain; add to it another and rather more modern paradox, borrowed by the Bohemian Lafontaine from the Bohemian Villon. If they are to be believed, the grasshopper, which dances and sings, has a better heart than the thrifty and laborious ant. True goodness, true pity, are found not in the labouring man, who sweats and strives all day in workshop or office, but in the vagabond who prefers a life of contemplation, feasts his eyes on the blue sky, and indolently exposes his body to the biting wind as readily as to the caressing summer breeze. He has nothing, yet he is ready to share everything, a curious kind of logic, the irony of which seems to escape some minds. On these two fascinating delusions, the virtue of primitive folk and the charity of vagabonds,

M. Jean Richepin has founded all his dramas, especially his famous *Chemineau.*

At length arose a young poet, the Edmond Rostand whom I mentioned just now. He asked nothing from anyone else. He simply said to himself that a drama, into which he could throw his passion, his intellect and his youth, all the poetry with which he was overflowing, would be a magnificent drama, a drama sparkling with fireworks. He wrote *Cyrano de Bergerac*, and carried it to Coquelin, who accepted it and put it upon the stage, with what success you know already.

We have had, therefore, plays hailing from every part of the literary horizon, and springing from the most diverse sources. Beware of applying a uniform code of criticism to them, or of judging them *à priori* according to the ideas which I have just summarised, and which merely serve as a point of departure. Do not attempt, moreover, to guess which have succeeded and which have failed; you will probably get wrong. Many of the plays were coldly received and promptly forgotten, some had a partial success, others were received with transports of enthusiasm. Why ?

A question of talent, that is all, neither a question of method nor of school. *Spiritus fiat ubi vult.* Now and again, a piece founded upon a vague or false conception, a work of art with most obvious defects, has produced, and still produces, an immense effect. Simply because the author, in certain parts of it, has introduced the kind of poetry calculated to stir an assemblage of several hundreds of people, to awaken in them that fleeting sense of the exquisite and the sublime which belongs to the music of the great masters, when sung by great artists. It is this which raises *Le Chemineau* of Richepin and the *Cyrano* of Rostand above their compeers.

The sun of Africa shone upon M. Jean Richepin in his cradle. Then the vicissitudes of life transported him to one of those Flemish cities, sleeping under their belfry towers, which have been so admirably described in English by Walter Pater, and by George Rodenbach amongst ourselves. At first he followed beaten tracks, and was a show pupil at the Lycée of Douai, where they still preserve some pages of his work, more

estimable than admirable. He next entered the
Ecole Normale, perhaps the least favourable soil
in the world for the cultivation of poets, plants
which can only grow like wild flowers under the
free air of heaven. After his school days, M.
Richepin tried several short cuts to glory, and
created a legend before he had achieved a reputation. The *brasseries* of the Quartier Latin were
wont to see him in strange guise, with velvet
coat, red silk sash, close-fitting breeches, high
boots and soft felt hat. As ring-master, gymnast,
amateur athlete, he is said to have accompanied
a travelling circus on its provincial tours, and
to have drawn crowds by certain exceptional
"turns." He wrote a play called *Nana Sahib*
for Sarah Bernhardt, which was sufficiently
worthless, but he had it played at the Porte
Saint Martin, and in the embroidered tunic of a
Hindoo prince, he expired every evening on the
top of a funeral pyre, in the arms of the famous
tragédienne. Then he went home, asked his
wife's pardon, and for a year or two seemed to
wish to be forgotten. But on the contrary, this
retreat merely set a seal upon the legend. There

are some people who would even enter the monastery of La Trappe, if they thought that it would be a good advertisement, and who keep silence simply to get themselves talked about. Some day I intend to collect all these recipes and to publish them as a set of maxims, *L'Art d'être célèbre* by an *Inconnu*.

But it is not enough to collect a crowd of fools round one by more or less wilful eccentricity. If one has nothing to show them, they go off in a huff and are in no hurry to come back. Happily this was not M. Richepin's fate. He might have dressed like you and me, he might have gone to bed at ten o'clock, got up at six, and taken his *déjeuner* and his dinner at regular hours; none the less he would have been a great poet, the poet of *Les Gueux* and *La Mer*. Perhaps even a greater, for all his fire, his passion, his intellectual electricity would have been kept for his verses.

He wrote some novels, which I beg to be excused from admiring. They annoy me by a deplorable mixture of the most outrageous realism with an idealism, which amounts to madness.

They are symbolism *sauce Zola*. As to M. Richepin's plays, up to now they have been little more than attempts at melodrama, with here and there flashes of poetry. But suddenly, in *Le Chemineau*, M. Richepin compelled both the friends and the enemies of his genius to join in a chorus of admiration. Like everybody else, I succumbed to the extraordinary charm of the play, and wondered all the time what it was that delighted me.

The harvest is coming to an end on Maître Pierre's farm. All has gone very well, thanks to a devil of a fellow, whose songs and jests have kept every one in good humour. Whence does he come? from everywhere and nowhere. What is he called? He has no name—he is simply le Chemineau.

"Oui, Chemineau, pas plus ! Un passant, un bonhomme
Qui mène tout, la joie et la peine, en chantant."

Yes, and the pain of other people too. Toinette, the little servant of Maître Pierre, has not been able to steel her heart against him. When the harvest is over, the insinuating vagabond departs with his eternal song on his lips, and the poor deserted girl would have been left to bear her grief and her added load of shame, had not François, the head servant, an honest fellow with whitening hair, come forward to protect her and to be a father to the Chemineau's child.

Life has now become unexpectedly sweet to Toinette. Her son has grown up into a good workman. He cultivates the land in the place of François, who is chained to his chair by paralysis. All would be well if Toinette's son and Maître Pierre's daughter had not taken it into their heads to fall in love. Maître Pierre is wealthy, proud, and avaricious. Not only will he never consent to the marriage, but he has sworn to ruin François and all his family. Toinet, in despair, frequents the wine shops, and the house, so long peaceful and prosperous, is filled with gloom. At this moment the Chemineau reappears, brought back by chance to the place, which he does not recognise. The sight of the misfortunes, of which he was the cause, awakens in him first memory, then tenderness, then conscience, and lastly, a wish to do right.

How will he manage to get over Maître Pierre? Partly by doing him a service, partly by intimidating him, for the Chemineau can play the sorcerer to perfection. So well, indeed, that in a trice the lovers are married, Toinette is com-forted, and old François dies in peace. A noble opportunity for the Chemineau to become a good peasant like the rest, and to find his happiness amongst the happy. A fine idea! and what about the great high road which is ever calling him and drawing him with a resistless fascina-tion? On a certain Christmas Eve, whilst the women are at the midnight mass, and a fat goose is roasting on the hearth for the watchnight supper, whilst the waits outside are singing carols, the wanderer slips out into the night:—

"Va Chemineau, chemine."

He must work out his destiny to the end, he can only stop to die.

That is the play. Its subject is one which would be readily accepted, but not exactly hailed as a "find." The secret of its success must, therefore, be sought elsewhere. Perhaps I was

U

the victim of the actors' art? Certainly the Odéon Company has not for years back appeared to greater advantage than in *Le Chemineau*. Still, it did not contain any of those sovereign artists who rivet the spectator and make him for the moment suspend any thought of criticism. What made me unhesitatingly accept those fictions, which do not convince me, that primitive goodness, that innate poetry, that deep simple soul of the people, in which I do not believe, in which no one believes? How could I ever listen for a moment to those peasants talking in verse, still less be moved by their talk? I wonder, I ask myself the question, and even when I find the answer, I am still more surprised than before. M. Richepin fairly got hold of me. He reduced my objections to nothing by employing those very methods which exasperated me in his novels, by combining idealism and realism. That is rather a humiliating discovery for the critics, and it ought to cure them of the exaggerated confidence which they are tempted to repose in preconceived formulas. In the domain of literature, especially in that of poetical drama, there is no such thing as good or bad, it all depends upon the particular case and the hour. An old Vaudevilliste, who was helping me years ago to bolster up a scenario, and to whom I pointed out the absurdities that we should have to encounter, replied with a comic grimace, " Either one has talent, or one has not." Generally, it is the second alternative, one has no talent. But M. Richepin has talent, and that in no stinted measure.

First, there are his lines, miracles of flexibility and elasticity. They break at pleasure into as many fragments as there are syllables, to convey the rough, brutal, laconic speech of the peasant. They contain the most commonplace words, but in some marvellous way the poetry, instead of being vulgarised by them, simply ennobles them. The style has all the freedom of prose, but, nevertheless, it preserves all the dignity and grace of poetry ; in this poetry the two forms of art combine—Hugo joins hands with Zola.

It is an amphibious style. Sometimes it wades in the mud and picks its way through the filth of the farmyard ; then, with one stroke of its wings, it is soaring in mid-air and describing harmonious curves through infinite space. How can one justify these alternations? In the simplest way in the world. Poetry is the blossoming out of the soul under the influence of some great thought or strange emotion. Some of the characters of *Le Chemineau* have none but coarse and animal ideas, but the uprightness and devotion of François, the love felt by Toinette, in the first act for her lover, and in the subsequent acts for her son, make the expression of their sentiments rise imperceptibly with the sentiments themselves. As for the Chemineau himself, before I know anything about him, before he has appeared on the stage, even before the curtain rises, I have heard him singing, and I can guess the sort of creature I have to deal with. That clear, sympathetic, vibrating voice rising up into space is in itself a character, a psychological fact, and I have no difficulty in understanding it, although it is never explained to me. The author does not enter into any discussion; he does not try to persuade me that all who tramp the high road are like this. He knows that besides the vagabond who sings there is a vagabond whose one thought is to kill, and that between the two there are many poor commonplace devils not worth the trouble of describing. His Chemineau is an exception; he sins out of sensualism and does good out of pity, for is not pity another form of sensuality? He is the incarnation of idleness, not the idleness of the sluggard, but the idleness of the restless wanderer, consumed by an eternal thirst for the changing and the unknown. He is fated to be a mere creature of fantasy, living apart from reality, apart from duty. Need it surprise us that such a man talks like a poet? Why, he is poetry itself. Please call to mind that whatever theory you may cherish about the origin of the *Iliad* and the *Odyssey*, the Homeric poems were the work of one or of several vagabonds. Were not the Trouvères and the Troubadours vagabonds too? Was not Villon, Cervantes, or Burns a vagabond, each in his own fashion? Nay, may not Richepin himself, even in his riper years, feel sometimes a pang of longing for the freedom of the great high road?

The year 1897 did not close without bringing us a work as beautiful, perhaps more beautiful, which met with a reception still more enthusiastic, either because the author's youth awoke still higher hopes, or because the light of genius shone out with greater freedom and spontaneity than in *Le Chemineau.* I am speaking of *Cyrano de Bergerac*, the drama written for the Porte Saint Martin by M. Edmond Rostand.

M. Rostand is only twenty-nine years old. He is the son of a very distinguished journalist of Marseilles, Eugéne Rostand, who might have had a brilliant career in the Paris press. But he preferred to live in his native town, where he devoted himself to the study of economic and labour questions, and took a keen interest in everything which concerns local politics and the internal organization of a great city. Between whiles he amused himself by translating and editing Catullus, a very great poet, whom we made a mistake in ignoring, and who ought to be given a place of honour between Lucretius and Virgil. Catullus might be called the intellectual god-father of Edmond Rostand, and I recognise some of his gifts in his brilliant god-son.

Celebrity of the best kind was slow to find out the father at Marseilles; the son leapt at once out of his provincial obscurity into the most exclusive circle of Parisian literary fame. He was twenty years old when he issued his first volume of verse, *Les Musardises*. I was at that time critic to the *Revue Bleue*. The book was both impertinent and engaging, a mixture of carelessness and preciosity, but it was full of the joy of life and of love, and it brought with it a ray of the sun, which melted the ice of pessimism. The publishers had never sent me anything so young, so fresh, so living, and I was bold enough to say that it was the most brilliant poetical début which the public had witnessed since the far-off day when Alfred de Musset published *Les Contes d'Espagne*. They laughed at me then; now the eulogy appears almost inadequate. Since that time M. Rostand has had a charming comedy, *Les Romanesques*, played at the Théâtre Français, and *La Samaritaine*, which I mentioned just now, at the Renaissance.

Finally, on the 28th December, 1897, henceforth a date in literature, the Porte Saint Martin gave for the first time *Cyrano de Bergerac*, in which Paris was delighted to meet again the charming spirituality of Mdlle. Legault, and in which our great Coquelin found scope for his artistic faculties, his magnificent and faultless diction, his fire, his mischief, his restrained and trembling tenderness, his depth of feeling, and his dazzling irony.

It is almost impossible to describe in English the personality of the original De Bergerac, the most French of all the Frenchmen of his time. Brimful of cleverness but mad, commanding admiration yet grotesque, he is a caricature and a hero, he is the very form and feature of tragi-comedy. There is in him much both of Pierre Corneille and of Alexandre Dumas. If he had put his genius into his works we should have had it in its completeness, but he lived it instead of writing it, he lavished it without thought of the morrow in mad freaks, sublime caprices, and irresponsible outbursts, he squandered it in improvisations of which not a trace remains.

They have vanished like a rocket fired into space two hundred years ago. Yet, thanks to Edmond Rostand and thanks to Coquelin, he lives again, and once more showers madness and fireworks about him, *Ecce Cyrano redivivus.*

This wonderful creation is a feat in itself, but where is the drama? It consists entirely in the strange contrast presented by Cyrano's double nature. On the one hand the brave and tender heart, the tongue so marvellously quick in a fencing-match of words, the hand so skilful in the more deadly play of the sword. On the other hand the ridiculous face, the nose for children to mock at, Don Juan imprisoned in the skin of Quasimodo. To hear him is to love him, but to see him is to make love impossible. Well, then, to win love his mind must take the outward semblance of another. He will write the letters of a young and attractive rival to whom he lends all the magic of his imagination, all the fever of his passion. He will prompt him, he will speak for him in a nocturnal rendezvous, hidden in the shade of Roxana's balcony, and when the happy lover has scaled the balcony and clasped his mistress in his arms, the sound of their first kiss will be both his torture and his reward. The years pass, the handsome lover has died at the wars; Roxana—a widow who has never been wife—has taken refuge in a convent, where she finds her chief solace in talking with Cyrano of the dear departed. Poor Cyrano! He has become the shadow of himself, and the hand of death is already upon him. His brilliant gifts have faded, his proud and genial nature only shows itself in spasmodic efforts. Roxana has no great difficulty in winning from the dying man the secret of his deception. For a few moments, then, he will be loved, or rather it was he who was always loved under the outward form of the handsome Christian.

Is this really a dramatic subject? Is it not rather a dream, a subtle, impalpable fancy? The " something divine, light and winged," which, according to Plato, is poetry itself? Did it not require remarkable audacity to think of basing five acts upon such a slight foundation, and a supernatural skill as well as an insolent good fortune to succeed in the task? However that may be, the wager was played and won by M. Rostand. His play had nothing vague about it; the life in it is so overflowing that it would be enough for ten plays. The human heart, which we thought could hold no more secrets or surprises, has grown quite young again, although, as Labruyère says, men have been living and thinking for six thousand years. The play speaks a language, old and yet new, which we love both for what it reveals and for what it restores. A torrent of images evoked on the spur of the moment, a vein of poetry, so full of freshness and novelty, overwhelm and intoxicate us, whilst the gaiety of earlier days flashes out in brilliant phrases, and covers us with a shower of sparks. The nightmare of symbolism is put to flight, the northern mists break and roll back before the glorious rays of this Provençal sun, which gives back to France her very self, her own peculiar genius. I do not shrink from saying that *Cyrano* is France, France at her best, France at the culminating point of her genius.

Two masterpieces in the space of a few months,

after so many years of leanness, cannot but raise innumerable hopes. One fact is henceforth certain. We have dramatic poets, and we have also a public for dramatic poetry.

So that the signs of renewal are appearing on all sides, and the transformation of the theatre is advancing so rapidly that new life is now making itself felt in the very places where, less than a year ago, I could discern only routine, discouragement, and inertia. Nor is this only true of the *théâtres à côté*, as people used to call the Théâtre Libre, and the other institutions created in imitation of it; but the regular legitimate theatres, open to the general public, are to-day full of promise and movement. The spirit of initative and of progress, sometimes perhaps a little subversive in its eagerness, but always well-intentioned, has penetrated into the old-established precincts, where nothing had moved for twenty years, and where tradition reigned supreme. There is movement in every direction, from the present towards both the future and the past, from the native drama towards the works of foreigners. Never have the classics been more piously performed. Not only do the two great houses devoted to classical drama never forget to keep the birthdays of Corneille, Racine, and Molière, like those of old and dearly-loved kinsmen, but the popular theatres have now their classical matinées, in which the *nouvelles couches* gain acquaintance with our masterpieces. Every week sees the unearthing of a forgotten comedy or drama, accompanied by an explanatory lecture. At the same time the old wall of prejudice against foreign dramatists begins to give way on every side, without, however letting in a rush of sentiment which would be fatal. The Odéon played Lytton's *Richelieu*, and the world did not laugh as much as I had feared. The Renaissance offered its audience the first taste of Gabriele d'Annunzio's *Ville Morte*, and the world did not yawn more than it had a right to do. The Théâtre de l'Œuvre gave two plays of Ibsen, *Jean Gabriel Borckmann* and *Rosmersholm* this year, as well as Gogol's *Rivizor* in Mérimée's translation. If the International Theatre succeeds in coming into being, it promises us the most interesting plays produced during the last few years by Spanish, Italian, and English dramatists.

The Théâtre Antoine has lowered the price of its seats, and this enables a new class of spectators to gain acquaintance with the best plays produced during the ten years at the Théâtre Libre. Its " soirées d'avant garde " will go on making experiments in new forms of art, so as to be in the forefront of discovery. The old theatres have not abandoned the long runs, which are so justly denounced on both sides of the Channel; but they now interrupt them by varied spectacles, and divide them by subscription nights, which tend to foster a special répertoire and a special public, like those of the Comédie Française and the Odéon. It is an excellent move, because it helps to give regularity and scope to the process of selection in these matters.

But the crowning fact to which I have striven to give prominence in this, my last study, is the revival of verse on the stage. And it is not only dramatic verse which is now flourishing in several theatres, lyrical verse has its share in this revival, and appropriates one evening a week at the Odéon. At the Bodinière it is quite at home, and although much that is impure mingles with the poetry in the amusement provided at the famous Butte, it must be recognised that poetry holds the first place there, and has become indispensable. A quarter of a century ago it would have been simply ignored, but from an outcast it has become a queen.

Some writers, even amongst our own countrymen, delight in bearing witness to the decay of the French mind, and in announcing the end of France. If I agreed with these prophets of misfortune, I should take care not to tell the English so. But, as a matter of fact, I am of an entirely different opinion. Whether it be a matter of rejoicing, or of affliction, France is in the best of health, and, whatever the world may say, shows no sign of mental disease. I cannot discern the dismal symptoms which are described with such melancholy pleasure, or if I do discern them, they seem to me unimportant, or even if a few of them are important, they are counterbalanced by reassuring phenomena. In the sphere of the drama, I have spoken of schools which are in process of dissolution, of worn-out systems, of principles which have lost their virtue, of old truths which have almost become false-hoods; but I have also pointed to rising talents, to new forces which are making themselves felt, to rich and fruitful combinations of ideas. It was in the autumn of 1895 that Dumas fils was taken from us. What a host of emotions and of discoveries have come to light since that date. On the one hand a long and brilliant series of experiments in the domain of comedy, of successes attained by young masters, whom no one had heard of eight years ago. On the other hand the unexpected revival of the drama brought about by our great poets, until it is more popular in all its forms than it ever was before. Verily, there is something here more than consolation, and more than promise. One thing is dying another is born, and there is nothing to prove that the dawning life may not equal, or even excel, that which is drawing to a close.